SURVIVAL TAILS

WORLD WAR II

SURVIVAL TAILS

WORLD WAR II

Book 3

By Katrina Charman

LITTLE, BROWN AND COMPANY
NEW YORK BOSTON

Copyright © 2019 by Katrina Charman
Illustrations copyright © 2019 by Owen Richardson

Cover art copyright © 2019 by Owen Richardson. Cover design by Kelly Brennan. Cover copyright © 2019 by Hachette Book Group, Inc.

Little, Brown and Company
Hachette Book Group
1290 Avenue of the Americas, New York, NY 10104
Visit us at LBYR.com

First Edition: October 2019

Little, Brown and Company is a division of Hachette Book Group, Inc. The Little, Brown name and logo are trademarks of Hachette Book Group, Inc.

The publisher is not responsible for websites (or their content) that are not owned by the publisher.

Library of Congress Cataloging-in-Publication Data
Names: Charman, Katrina, author.
Title: World War II / by Katrina Charman.
Other titles: World War Two
Description: First edition. | New York; Boston : Little, Brown and Company, 2019. | Series: Survival tails; book 3 | Summary: "A group of brave zoo animals must survive the London Blitz during World War II"— Provided by publisher. | Includes bibliographical references.
Identifiers: LCCN 2019012142| ISBN 9780316477932 (trade pbk.) | ISBN 9780316477949 (ebook) | ISBN 9780316477918 (library edition ebook)
Subjects: LCSH: Britain, Battle of, Great Britain, 1940—Juvenile fiction. | CYAC: Britain, Battle of, Great Britain, 1940—Fiction. | World War, 1939–1945—Great Britain—Fiction. | Homing pigeons—Fiction. | Pigeons—Fiction. | London Zoo (London, England)—Fiction. | Zoo animals—Fiction. | Animals—Fiction. | Survival—Fiction.
Classification: LCC PZ7.1.C495 Wor 2019 | DDC [Fic]—dc23
LC record available at https://lccn.loc.gov/2019012142

ISBNs: 978-0-316-47793-2 (pbk.), 978-0-316-47794-9 (ebook)

Printed in the United States of America

LSC-C

10 9 8 7 6 5 4 3 2 1

For Maddie, Piper, and Riley.
In loving memory of my nan and grandad.

CHAPTER 1
FRANCIS

September 5, 1940
Normandy, France

Francis stalked back and forth inside his coop, trying not to jump whenever a flash of light illuminated the night sky, or the *rat-tat-tat* of gunfire pierced the rare moments of silence. He supposed that he should be used to it, the sound of war, but now that he was the only pigeon in his division, he couldn't distract himself by chatting with the others.

It was worse for the humans. The latest Nazi attack had been going on for weeks with no end in sight, and the men had little time for rest or food before another round of fighting began. The enemy was moving closer.

Gaining ground. Soon the British troops and their allies would have to retreat or...Francis couldn't bring himself to think of the alternative.

The coop door swung open, startling Francis, as George, the pigeon handler, threw a handful of seed inside. George gently stroked Francis's head. It had an immediate calming effect, as it always did. Francis turned his attention to his meal, frantically scooping seed into his beak until he remembered that he didn't have to race anymore. There were no other pigeons to tussle with.

"Slow down," George chided. "You'll be no good to us if you choke on a sunflower seed."

Francis glanced guiltily up at George and opened his beak, releasing his stash of seeds to the floor.

"It's going to be a long night," George said, pulling the collar of his heavy green jacket up around his ears.

Francis cooed in agreement. Even though summer had barely passed, the war seemed to have brought with it a creeping chill that wove its way through camp and sent a shiver through Francis's feathers. His ears were constantly ringing with the echoes of gunfire. He ignored his food and hopped closer to George.

"At least I've still got you to take my mind off things," George said, gently lifting Francis out of the coop and warming him close to his chest.

They stood in silence as the assaults continued in the distance. Francis felt George's heart beating rapidly within his chest, matching his own quick breaths.

"I wonder how long we have left," George whispered.

Francis felt his stomach drop. Every soldier—man and pigeon—knew what they had signed up for when they joined the war. Knew that there was always the chance that each day might be their last. It didn't make it any less scary, though.

George gave a small huff of a laugh, then put Francis back inside the coop. "Well, you'll be getting out of this hole soon enough at least. And I'll…" He trailed off, and Francis rubbed his head against George's hand, comforting his friend in the only way he could.

"Any day now, I expect," George said. "You'll be off on your first official mission."

Francis puffed up his chest at this. He'd been preparing his whole life to be sent on a mission. Now that he was the last pigeon left, he was sure to be chosen soon. The thought sent a flutter of both excitement and dread through his feathers. But then he saw the pained expression on George's face and for the first time understood what that would really mean, having to leave his friend behind.

George mustered up a cheery smile. "Well, let's spend what little time we have left together. Good night, Francis."

"Good night, George," Francis cooed back.

George closed the coop, then settled down beside it, resting his dark green metal helmet over his face. Within minutes, he was snoring. Francis wondered how George could sleep so easily with so much going on around them. But he was glad of his company, even though George was a human. Francis had to admit that he could rest easier when George was close by.

He finished the last of the seed, then pecked at his blue-gray feathers, grooming himself to make sure his wings were in the best possible condition. It had been a while since he'd been allowed out of his coop to fly any kind of distance, and his wings felt stiff. He hoped he wouldn't let George down when the time came to leave.

He put the thought out of his mind, instead busying himself with collecting straw and plucked feathers into a pile, making a cozy nest in the corner of the coop. He buried himself inside, hoping to block out some of the noise, or at least the cold.

He had just closed his eyes when a loud voice startled him.

"What news?" the voice demanded from behind the coop. Francis recognized it as the lieutenant general's.

Francis poked his head out of his cocoon and peered through the wire mesh. At first he thought the lieutenant general had been talking to George, but his keeper slept on, oblivious. Francis didn't recognize the man who stood with him, disheveled and out of breath, but he knew the lieutenant general himself well enough. Francis had been stationed with him and his troops since they had arrived in Normandy a few months ago.

"We've had word from one of our intelligence officers on the German border that Hitler has a new plan to attack Britain," the other man wheezed. Blood trickled down his face from beneath his helmet, dripping into his eye, and his uniform was ripped and muddied. "I came as fast as I could to get the message to you, sir. Didn't even stop when the Nazis started shooting at me."

The camp was surrounded by twisting, razor-sharp wire and defense walls built out of everything from broken carts to pews from the local church. Francis wondered how the soldier had made it past the enemy.

"When?" the lieutenant general whispered, glancing around to make sure that no one else was listening.

That was one of the advantages of being a pigeon. Humans could say anything around Francis and not give it a second thought. *Never mind messenger pigeons*, he thought, *they should have spy pigeons*. Although there was the tiny issue of how the pigeon could then relay their intelligence—information that they had discovered about the enemy—back to the humans, but still. Francis knew he would make an excellent spy.

"Soon, sir," the soldier replied in equally hushed tones. "The Nazis are calling it Operation Sea Lion. They plan to attack from the air. They have already targeted our defenses along the south coast of England, and the Royal Air Force bases. Once those are disabled, they will attack London."

"A blitzkrieg," the lieutenant general said, his face as white as the moon above.

A sudden shudder ran through Francis. He had heard that word spoken in whispers at night, when both sides were tending to their wounded. Except the men didn't use the full German word. They simply called it a blitz—a lightning war. An attack that destroyed everything and anything in its path and could bring Britain to its knees.

"Private Morgan!" the lieutenant general yelled, walking around the coop to kick George's boot to wake him.

George was up in an instant. "Yes, sir! Just checking on the pigeon, sir!"

He grabbed a handful of straw and opened the coop to shove it right into Francis's face. George had been trying to keep as busy as possible, or at least make it look that way. Because as soon as George was no longer required as a pigeon handler, he would be sent away to fight. That was something that neither Francis nor George wanted, so Francis began scratching at the wooden floor of the coop, making as much fuss as a pigeon could make in the middle of a war zone.

"Private," the lieutenant general started, then paused as he peered into the coop. "What the devil is wrong with the pigeon?"

"Nothing, sir," George replied quickly, giving Francis a nervous glance. "It's just the noise of the..." He waved his hand in the air, gesturing at nothing in particular.

The lieutenant general frowned. "I need to send an urgent message to Bletchley," he said. "But if the pigeon is not able to handle a few loud noises..." He trailed off, eyeing Francis warily.

Francis stood to attention. He didn't want George to be sent to the front line, but neither did he want the lieutenant general to think he wasn't up for the job. His father and grandfather before him had been carrier pigeons. His great-great-great-grandfather had served in the First World War. Using pigeons to carry important messages was the quickest and most efficient way for the humans to communicate during the war. It was an honor for Francis to do the same. He wouldn't bring shame upon his family by letting the humans believe he wasn't up to the task.

George gave Francis a small nod, then turned to the lieutenant general. "He's more than capable, sir," George replied. "He's the best pigeon I've ever looked after. That's why I saved him till last."

Francis watched George, wondering if that was true. George had always been kind to him, but he treated all of the pigeons well. Francis hadn't realized that was the reason he had been left behind to watch his friends fly off into danger.

The lieutenant general peered at Francis again, who stood stock-still, terrified and excited all at once, afraid to even blink.

"Very well," he said finally. "I suppose he is our only option anyway. We are all but surrounded by the enemy and this message needs to get to Britain immediately."

He pulled out a small pad of paper and a pencil from the breast pocket of his jacket and scribbled a note. He held it out of George's sight so that he couldn't read it, but Francis could. There was a series of numbers and letters. He recognized it as an encrypted code that the British army used for all the messages they sent. Should the worst happen and the messenger was caught, the enemy would be unable to decipher the message.

The lieutenant general rolled the paper into a cylinder, and George handed him a small scarlet-colored capsule no bigger than his little finger. The note was carefully eased into the capsule, then sealed with a lid. George opened the coop and Francis stepped forward, allowing him to attach the capsule to his leg.

George paused for a moment, his eyes shining as he stroked Francis's head. Francis cooed quietly in response, wishing that he could say a real goodbye— to thank George for all that he had done these last few months, caring for him and making him feel safe in a place where *safe* was an almost impossible word. To say that he hoped to see George again someday. But all he could do was coo and hope that George understood.

"Take this home," George told him. "As quickly as you can." He gave Francis a small smile. "I'll miss you. Stay safe, my friend."

Francis bobbed his head, then spread his wings, praying that they were ready for the long, dangerous journey ahead. He glanced back at George one last time, then took off, soaring up and over the enemy, hoping that the darkness would keep him hidden from view as he headed toward the code-breaking facility at Bletchley.

His home.

CHAPTER 2

MING

September 7, 1940
London Zoo, England

Ming chewed slowly on a thick bamboo shoot, watching from the shadows of her enclosure as the humans peered through the thick metal bars for a glimpse of the *famous* giant panda. She couldn't understand what all the fuss was about. When she'd arrived at the zoo as a cub, the zookeepers had built a raised wooden platform in the middle of the enclosure, with two planks on either side for her to climb up and down onto it. But Ming didn't understand what they expected her to do. She couldn't perform tricks like the monkeys, and she wasn't fierce or loud like the lions. She certainly couldn't take children for rides around the grounds like the elephants.

She was just an ordinary giant panda. No different than the other giant pandas roaming the bamboo forests of China. Except Ming wasn't in China anymore, and she certainly wasn't in a forest.

"They won't come back if you ignore them," Tang grumbled beside her, nodding to the final visitors for the day. "They want to see the zoo's *star attraction*."

Ming ignored Tang and the pointing humans who called her name, and continued chomping on her bamboo. She wanted to ask Tang why *he* didn't go out there instead, but she stayed quiet. He was a giant panda, too. Why was it always *her* the humans wanted to see? She sighed and picked up another bamboo shoot. She knew the answer, of course. It was because she was the first—the first giant panda ever to have been seen in London. Well, the first giant panda ever to have been seen *alive*.

The thought of it made her queasy.

Behind her, the metal bolt on the door to the enclosure slid open, and a slightly sweaty and red-faced Jean appeared, holding up a bucket of bamboo. She was smaller than the average adult human, with short brown hair that she swept behind her ears. As usual, she wore oversized dark blue overalls with the sleeves and legs rolled up several times so that it fit her properly. They were covered in dark brown splotches of what Ming hoped was just mud.

"Phew!" the zookeeper puffed. "I just cleaned out the camels' enclosure. Trust me, that is not fun!"

She smiled as she saw Ming and Tang, then emptied out the bucket of bamboo onto the ground. "There's not a lot today, I'm afraid," Jean said. "We're running low on everything."

Ming crinkled her nose and sniffed at the bamboo. Since the humans' war had started, Jean and the other keepers had had no choice but to find food for the animals closer to home. They had closed their sister zoo, Whipsnade, and used half of its land to grow produce for the animals and humans. Just as the humans' food was rationed, so was the animals'. Now, instead of their usual bamboo imported from China, Ming and Tang were fed shoots that had been grown in Cornwall.

They tasted different. Bitter.

The old bamboo tasted like home. And now that her memories of home and family were fading faster every day, bamboo was the last connection she had to them.

"Looks like you've got a crowd," Jean said to Ming,

stroking her head. "Why don't you go and say hello to your fans?"

Tang snorted. "Ming won't even talk to me, let alone her *fans*."

Ming turned to scowl at Tang. "That's because you have nothing interesting to say."

Tang raised his eyebrows. "And the humans do, I suppose?"

Ming didn't have an answer to that. Aside from Jean, Ming didn't really care much for the humans either way. Urged on by Jean, she lumbered toward the front of her enclosure. Despite what Jean had said, the crowd was smaller than usual, and Ming noticed that there were only a few children. Jean had told them that many of London's children had already been evacuated to the countryside, in the hopes of keeping them safer from the Nazi attacks.

"You too, Tang," Jean encouraged, giving him a gentle push on his behind. "Don't let Ming steal the limelight."

Tang huffed and followed after Ming to excited gasps from the crowd.

"Would you look at that," a man said, pushing a

little redheaded girl forward to stand right at the front. He wore a shabby gray cap, and Ming noticed that the right sleeve of his jacket hung empty, his arm most likely lost due to a war injury.

The little girl waved at Ming, then held up a small stuffed toy panda.

"Look, Ming," she said, bobbing the stuffed panda up and down. "It's you!" The girl held the toy up to the bars and laughed. "Ming, meet Ming!"

Ming eyed the stuffed toy panda suspiciously. It looked nothing like her—more like a deformed badger than a panda—but the toys made Tang jealous, so Ming always made a point of showing off to the crowd whenever she spotted one. Or at least she did the best she could do at showing off, which was mainly sitting and eating her bamboo closer to the humans.

Beside her, Tang huffed again and Ming smiled a little, despite there being so many eyes watching her.

"Don't just sit there and stare at them," Tang said. "They are here for a show. That's why they brought us back from Whipsnade Zoo after being evacuated— to bring back the crowds. Watch this..." Tang lay on the floor, then rolled over onto his back. The little girl clapped her hands, and Tang gave Ming a triumphant look.

Rolling is not much of a skill, Ming thought. She turned her back on the crowd and headed back to Jean. Ming wished she were still at Whipsnade. She had liked it there. It was quiet and peaceful, with no crowds, and she hadn't felt as though she were on display all day long.

Ming watched Jean sweep the floor as Tang did another roll, almost knocking her over.

"It looks like Tang is having fun," Jean teased, leaning on her broom. "Why don't you join him?"

Ming sniffed, then picked up a bamboo shoot and slowly chewed at the end to show Jean what she thought about her suggestion.

"You might enjoy it if you give it a go," Jean said. She shook her head and continued sweeping, a small smile on her face.

The smile quickly dropped as a screaming sound filled the air.

Sirens.

Ming's heart beat out of her chest as the humans scattered in all directions. In the panic, the little girl dropped her stuffed Ming toy.

"Daddy!" she screamed at her father. "My Ming!"

He ignored her pleas and pulled a heavy black gas mask with big goggled eyes down over her face, then carried her away to the closest air-raid shelter, her cries muffled beneath the mask.

"Inside!" Jean shouted at Ming and Tang, herding them beneath the covered part of the enclosure. "I'll be back as soon as I can."

She raced out of the enclosure, slamming the door shut.

Ming glanced at Tang. His eyes matched her own— wide and afraid as the sirens wailed on, warning that something bad was approaching.

"It will be all right," Tang whispered over and over again. "We'll be all right. Everything will be all right."

Tang's fear hung in the air between them like a smothering cloud. Ming's fur was on edge, hackles raised. Her heart raced, and all the while chaos filled the zoo. Worse, even, than the sounds of the sirens were the sounds that filled her head. The screaming monkeys and braying zebras. The birds in the aviaries, squawking and flying at the wire mesh again and again, trying to break free.

Ming squeezed her eyes shut, and a memory flashed before her. Her mother calling out for her as the humans came with nets and cages. While other animals ran away and the men gave chase, Ming could do nothing but sit, frozen, even though her mother urged her to run and hide. She couldn't. She couldn't leave her only family. So she sat and watched until the men took her, too.

She forced down a sob and moved closer to Tang, covering her ears with her paws to block out the terrible sound, but she could still feel the vibrations of the noise. A couple of zookeepers ran past, making sure that all the humans had left, and Ming was dismayed to see Jean with them.

"She should be in the shelter!" Tang cried, echoing Ming's own fears.

Ming watched Jean, Ming's entire body clutched by terror, until she saw her keeper head off in the direction of the offices where the humans sheltered in the basement.

But for the animals, for Ming and Tang and all the others, there was nowhere to run to. Nowhere to hide. There was nothing to do but sit and await their fate. Just like she had done in China.

She shuffled herself farther into the corner of the enclosure, trying to make her huge body as small as possible, waiting for the raid to pass. Sometimes it was a false alarm, and the humans returned almost as quickly as they had left. But other times... other times it continued on into the night, while the animals sat in the absolute darkness, watching, and waiting, and hoping, that the flying beasts stayed away. That they wouldn't drop their bombs. That they wouldn't fall near the zoo.

"M-Ming," Tang stammered, "I'm afraid."

"Me too," Ming whispered, too quietly for Tang to hear.

Finally, as the sky darkened, the wailing sirens wound down. Ming craned her neck forward a little to look out to the sky above and see if it was clear. But no sooner had the sirens stopped when they started up again, and accompanying them, a new, even more terrifying noise. It began as a low hum, barely noticeable if you weren't listening carefully. But then the sound grew, like a swarm of angry bees protecting their queen, rising into a crescendo until the mechanical motors were all you could hear.

Nazi bombers.

Ming caught sight of them in the distance. The planes flew in a V formation, like a flock of geese, gliding low over London, seeking out their targets. Gunfire echoed around the city, then *thud*, *thud*, *thud*s in quick succession as the bombs landed. There was a pause, no longer than an intake of breath, before snaking trails of black smoke rose high into the sky. The bombers had found their targets. Somewhere close, buildings were burning.

Ming was breathing so hard she felt as though her chest would explode like one of those bombs.

"Oh no," Tang whispered beside her.

She followed Tang's gaze. The planes that had passed over them turned in the sky, still in formation.

They were headed right for the zoo.

CHAPTER 3
FRANCIS

September 7, 1940

The south coast of England came into view as the sun began to set. Francis had flown all night and into the next day without stopping, and now his wings felt like they were made of rubber and his lungs were on fire. Still, he pushed himself on, focusing on the looming white cliffs of Dover running as far as he could see in either direction. Finally, he swooped up and over the cliff tops, then soared over a field as yellow as the sun itself.

He landed among the mustard-yellow flowers of the rapeseed and allowed himself a moment to rest and get his bearings, snatching up an unsuspecting worm as it chose the wrong moment to poke its head up out of the soil. Francis preferred seed, which didn't wriggle its way down his throat like the worm, but it had been so long since he'd eaten that he couldn't afford to be fussy.

The coastline was reinforced with defenses. Metal posts entwined with barbed wire and hidden mines jutted out of the sea along the beach to deter enemy ships attempting to reach land. Farther along where the beach became wider, huge concrete blocks had been placed so that enemy ships that did make it to shore would be unable to offload their tanks.

Francis slowed, carefully scanning the land ahead in all directions, alert. There was a sudden release of gunfire, and Francis dropped just in time, narrowly avoiding being shot out of the sky. Luckily, this was what he had been anticipating, had been trained to do. He flew low, trying to identify where the gunfire had come from, then he saw it.

A pillbox.

A squat concrete building, with only the narrowest of windows. They were meant for the humans to fire machine guns through and shoot down anything that looked even slightly suspicious in the sea or sky. Although he was flying over his home territory, Francis was still keenly aware of the potential dangers.

The British RAF Spitfires were easily recognizable with painted circles on their tails and beneath their wings. The Home Guard manning the defenses wouldn't dare to shoot down one of their own, but pigeons like Francis had no markings. They all looked the same to the humans, and the gunmen below had no idea whether he was friend or foe. All they knew was that if there was the possibility that Francis might be carrying a message for the other side, especially if they spotted the bright red canister tied to his leg, they might chance it and shoot him down anyway.

As Francis flew closer, the gunfire came again, but this time he was ready. He easily dodged the bullets, then moved into position so that he still had the pillbox in his sights, but the sniper within was no longer able to see him through his narrow window at the angle he was flying.

Francis passed safely out of range, then let himself relax a little.

He scanned the area one last time in case there were more hidden pillboxes. Then he flew on, ignoring the pain that screamed through his shoulders.

He turned west for London, desperate for water and a chance to sleep, but he knew he didn't have the time.

He would sleep once he'd delivered the message. It was far more important than his own needs, and he refused to let George or his country down.

As he continued his journey, the sun was disappearing on the horizon. In training, when Francis had flown to London before, he had seen the bright lights of the city from miles away. But this time, the city was in darkness, as though he were still flying over the ocean. Despite his excellent homing instincts, he faltered for a moment, reminding himself that it was only dark because of the blackouts. The humans kept all lights to an absolute minimum. Besides, he told himself, that was a good thing. He could fly undetected. And if a pigeon with his superior navigating skills was finding it difficult to locate London, then the Nazis would have an even harder task.

Still, he couldn't shake the growing unease bubbling up inside him as he flew on blindly. The Luftwaffe— the German air force—were notorious for night raids. That meant that the danger shifted from the ground to the sky, Francis's territory. He would likely have to fly on through the night, pass over London, and then head north to Bletchley. He hoped that there were no air raids planned.

He continued on, pushing his wings to their limit, knowing he had to keep going. Then he heard it, long before it came into view.

A German Messerschmitt! The looming shadow of the fighter plane crept over him as it flew overhead. Francis's heart raced faster as he somehow found a little more strength within to push even harder and stay steady on his course. There was nothing else he could do but fly on beneath the enemy planes. Francis thought of George and the lieutenant general and the soldier who had risked his life to get the message to them. He couldn't let them down. He *wouldn't*. Not when he had already come so far. Not when Bletchley was only a few hours away.

It was an important place, where only the best code breakers worked night and day, decoding messages and data, helping the British forces and their allies stay one step ahead of the enemy. He had been born at Bletchley, like his mother and father and grandparents before him. Entire generations of pigeons bred to be more than just birds—to be heroes.

In the distance, the silhouette of the dome of Saint Paul's Cathedral rose into view, backed by a giant smear of oranges, pinks, and reds across the sky as the sun set behind it. Below, air-raid sirens wailed their warnings in unison across the city. The sight of it gave Francis renewed energy. He would not let the enemy win.

Heavy black vapor streams filled the air as the planes dropped lower, making it even harder to see. Francis coughed, choking on fumes as the air filled with thick smoke. In his panic, he stopped flapping for a moment and his stomach dropped as he fell toward the ground. He forced his wings to move even though he couldn't see where he was going and could barely catch his breath.

He dove lower, hoping to come out of the smog, but as soon as the air cleared a little, he came face-to-face with a giant beast. He swerved, narrowly avoiding a collision with a bulbous barrage balloon. These large balloons were tethered all over the city to keep the enemy bombers high, to stop them from getting too close. They looked to Francis like a pod of whales bobbing in the air.

He took a deep gulp of fresh air and reset his course, feeling his nerves settle a little.

Then the shooting started.

Ahead, a Messerschmitt plummeted suddenly. It veered to the left but caught its wing on one of the barrage balloon's thick cables. Its entire left wing sheared off and the plane fell into a tailspin, exploding in a blast of blinding light and heat that erupted toward Francis.

He swerved to avoid being caught in the blast, straining to fly higher and higher. But his wings finally gave up on him. He froze in midair for a split second before he began to fall.

Down, down, down he went, as the world blurred around him in a whirl of fire and heat and noise.

And then there was nothing, nothing but the darkness.

CHAPTER 4
MING

September 7, 1940

Bright light filled the sky, temporarily blinding Ming. Although the plane had gone down outside of Regent's Park, Ming was sure she could feel the heat from the blast.

"What happened?" Tang squeaked beside her.

Ming shook her head, cautiously making her way out into the open to view the sky in all directions in case there were more planes coming. Aside from the blazing fire from the downed plane illuminating the darkness, she could see nothing.

"Please let Jean be all right," she whispered.

"Are they gone?" Tang asked, huddling in the corner of the enclosure.

Ming held her paw to her mouth to shush him, then listened. The noises from the zoo had settled slightly, but there was still the odd whimper or growl coming from the various enclosures. A faint buzzing sound came from the east. She turned in that direction and saw dark smudges in the sky, headed away from London. Whatever had caused the plane to crash must have scared the enemy away, Ming thought. They were safe... for now.

She moved to join Tang, when something else caught her eye, falling with increasing speed directly above her, leaving a wispy trail of smoke in its wake. It was too small to be a bomb and didn't come with the screaming noise of the incendiary bomb.

As it came clearer into view, Ming saw that it was a bird. She stepped out of the way, narrowly avoiding being hit as it crashed to the ground inside the enclosure.

Ming sat shocked for a moment, unable to move as she looked at the poor, broken thing that had almost killed her. It was in such a state that it was hard to tell what type of bird it might have been, but Ming guessed it was a pigeon. They were the most common birds found in Regent's Park, which surrounded the zoo. It must have been caught in the gunfire.

Ming took a breath to calm her racing heart and moved closer. "Oh no!" she whispered.

The pigeon lay awkwardly on the ground, its left wing bent at an unnatural angle. Gray and white feathers were scattered all around the bird. Its head faced away from her, so she couldn't see if its eyes were open or closed, and she wasn't sure she wanted to.

"Leave it alone!" Tang called from behind her. "There's nothing you can do for the wretched creature."

Ming looked back at Tang crinkling his nose in disgust. Then she turned toward the small, helpless bird who had been caught in the middle of the humans' war. It was no different than she and all the other animals in the zoo. Ming felt a flash of anger inside her. At least the humans had places to hide, ways to stay safe and protect themselves. The animals had nothing. They were little more than sitting targets, surrounded only by hope and fear.

The sky faded from black to an inky blue, then lilac as the sun rose, and Ming inched closer to the bird.

The pigeon's leg jolted suddenly, and Ming sprang back in surprise as it tried to lift its head.

"Stay still," Ming said, barely more than a whisper, amazed that the pigeon was somehow still breathing.

The pigeon groaned and lifted its head again, glancing down at its leg. "Message," he croaked.

Ming leaned in closer to try to understand what the pigeon was saying. Its eyes grew wide with terror as it saw her bearing down on him.

"Don't...eat...me!" he begged.

Tang chuckled. "Why would she want to eat you?"

The pigeon grew even more alarmed as Tang appeared beside Ming.

"Bears!" the pigeon squawked.

Tang tutted. "We are very rare and valuable giant pandas, not common *bears*!"

Ming nodded at the pigeon, backing away slightly to give him some space and to reassure him that she wasn't about to attack. "We are vegetarian," she said quietly. "We don't eat pigeons. Although...some giant pandas do eat meat, I suppose." She saw the look of horror on the pigeon's face and realized that she wasn't doing a very good job reassuring him.

She looked to Tang to say something helpful, but he was staring at her, his jaw hanging open in surprise.

"Th-that's the most I've ever heard you say in one go!" he stuttered. "All these years we've been living together, with only each other for company. And do I ever get a *Good morning, Tang* or *How are you today, Tang?* You barely even acknowledge Jean, and she's the only friend you've got in this place!"

Ming felt the blood drain from her face.

Tang paused. "Ming...I'm sorry. I didn't mean..."

"I don't need friends," Ming hissed under her breath. "Least of all you."

She turned back to the pigeon. He had somehow managed to stand despite his injuries and was now flapping his good wing while jumping, evidently trying to fly away, but failing terribly.

"Your wing is injured," Ming told him gently. "I think it might be broken. You shouldn't try to fly."

Tang nodded in agreement. "You're not going anywhere," he said.

"Maybe Jean will help?" Ming suggested. "She promised she'd come back as soon as she could."

The pigeon abandoned his futile attempts to fly and sank to the ground. "Who is Jean?"

"Our keeper," Ming said. "You'll like her, she—"

"Oh no!" the pigeon squawked. "No humans! I can't let any humans see my message. It's very important and top secret and—" He quickly snapped his beak shut. "I didn't tell you any of that—I must be delirious from my head injury. I am just an ordinary pigeon from the park."

As if to prove his point, he started cooing and pecking randomly at the ground, wincing each time he moved. One of his legs was redder than the other and seemed swollen. Ming narrowed her eyes as she examined it. It looked like some kind of canister or container was attached.

"What's that on your leg?" she asked.

The pigeon lifted his leg slightly, so that he looked like a balancing flamingo, covering it with his good wing. "Nothing," he said. "Nothing. Just a...um..." He sighed. "It contains a note," he admitted. "I am part of the NPS. That's the National Pigeon Service, to you civilians. My commanding officer is Lieutenant General Worthington and I have a very important message to deliver. The entire country is depending on me!" he said. "Or at least it was until that blasted Messerschmitt knocked me off course."

Ming frowned. "You won't be able to deliver it with a broken wing."

The pigeon looked at her desperately. "I must!" he

said. "Something terrible will happen if I don't. I was trusted with this mission and I cannot fail."

He examined the enclosure as though looking for an escape route. The bars were wide enough for him to fit through if he wanted to, and most of the enclosure was open air with no ceiling, but the pigeon seemed barely able to stand for longer than a few moments, let alone fly.

There was a rattle behind the enclosure, and the jangle of keys.

"Jean!" Ming cried, relief flooding through her that the keeper was okay. Despite her anger at Tang, he was right—Jean was her only friend in the zoo. "She can fix your wing, and then maybe you can deliver your note?"

The pigeon shook his head. "No, no, no! She might see the message. Rule number one: Trust no one. You never know who could be a spy for the enemy."

Tang snorted. "I can assure you that Jean is not a spy. Spies wouldn't spend their days cleaning up panda dung, for a start. They'd be doing much more interesting things, I imagine, like..."

"Spying?" Ming supplied.

Tang scowled at her.

"Please!" the pigeon begged Ming. "You have to help me remove the capsule and hide it somewhere. I have to keep the message safe."

Ming examined the red capsule. It was firmly attached to the pigeon's leg with a thick plastic binding. "I don't think it can be removed," she said. "At least not without human help."

The pigeon gazed beseechingly at Tang.

"I don't know what you expect me to do," Tang muttered, avoiding the pigeon's desperate eyes.

There was a clang as the thick metal enclosure door was unlocked, and then a swoosh as the heavy door was slid open.

"*Please!*" the pigeon wailed.

Without thinking, Ming lunged at the pigeon as though she was about to attack, her teeth bared. The pigeon reared back with a squawk as she clamped her jaws down onto the capsule.

"Stay still!" she mumbled through her closed jaw.

The pigeon relaxed a little as Ming started to grind her teeth back and forth over the capsule's binding as though it were a bamboo shoot, being careful not to injure the pigeon's leg.

The pigeon caught her eye and gave her a nervous smile. "I'm Francis, by the way," he said.

Finally, the capsule broke free. Ming quickly scooped it up and hid it beneath her paw as the keeper appeared.

Jean paused as she took in the sight of the bloodied, disheveled pigeon, her eyes filled with concern.

"Well," she said. "What do we have here?"

CHAPTER 5
FRANCIS

September 8, 1940

The zookeeper approached tentatively, kneeling down in front of Francis as she reached out to him.

"Poor thing," she said. "Looks like you've been shot out of the sky like a bomber plane."

Little does she know, Francis thought. She didn't seem to present any immediate danger, so he remained calm while the keeper gently lifted him up and carried him toward the gate at the back of the enclosure.

Ming followed anxiously. The keeper turned, puzzled. "It's all right," she told Ming. "I'm just going to fix him up."

"Keep the message safe for me until I get back," Francis whispered.

The keeper took him into a room behind the enclosure.

It was filled with crates full of bamboo. Charts hung along the walls, covered with scribbled notes about the giant pandas' diet, exercise, and any other information the humans felt necessary to record. Francis thought it must be awful having your every move monitored, never really being free to do what you wanted, go where you pleased. Although, he supposed, his life was much the same way. He belonged to the humans and did what they needed him to do, whenever they needed him to do it. His life was no more his own than Ming's was.

The zookeeper, Jean, placed him on the table and rummaged through some cupboards, producing a case full of various medical instruments and bottles of potions and lotions, a wad of bandages, and a roll of gauze.

She filled a bowl with water at the small sink in the corner of the room, then gently wiped Francis's feathers with cotton balls, being careful not to hurt him. Francis watched the water turn a murky pink color as Jean cleaned away the blood, and his stomach felt a little queasy.

"It looks worse than it is," Jean said. "You were lucky, little guy. You've got a few scrapes and grazes, but most of the damage is contained to your left wing."

She glanced at Francis. "This is going to hurt a little, I'm afraid."

Francis took a deep breath and closed his eyes. There was a gentle tug on his shoulder, then nothing. Francis opened one eye, surprised that it hadn't hurt as much as he'd thought it would, when Jean forcefully pushed his wing up and back into the socket, sending a fire burning through Francis worse than any explosion.

He shrieked in agony, but Jean held him close, stroking his head. "It's all over now," she told him. "You are a very brave pigeon."

"Jean?" a loud voice boomed from the doorway. "What do you have there?"

Jean's smile dropped from her face. "Sir...it's a pigeon; he somehow found his way into the pandas' enclosure. He's injured," she said quickly. "I was only—"

"You are not paid to look after *pigeons*," the boss growled.

"I'm a volunteer," Jean whispered under her breath. "I'm not paid at all."

"What was that?" the boss barked.

He was a short, stout man, with a graying beard and mustache and tufts of black hair that protruded from his nose and ears. His dark eyes flashed at Francis as he continued. "They are little more than flying rats. Get it out of here before it infects our animals with some hideous disease."

Jean lowered her head. "Yes, sir. I'll just bind his wing, then I'll take him away from the zoo."

The man gave a curt nod, then left.

"You're not vermin, are you?" she huffed, binding Francis's wing with the bandage a bit tighter than necessary. "You seem clean and well fed. I wonder where you've come from."

Francis avoided her gaze, trying to act like a normal, everyday pigeon. Maybe he wouldn't make a very good spy after all, if humans suspected him this easily.

"There," Jean said, tying off the ends of the bandage into a knot. "All done. You won't be able to fly for at least two weeks, though, I'm afraid."

She glanced at the door. "I can't just leave you out in the open to fend for yourself," she muttered. "The foxes will get you before you've had a chance to heal."

She picked him up and checked that the coast was clear before returning to Ming's enclosure. "Of course," she said aloud as she put Francis on top of a pile of straw in a corner of the enclosure. "I have no control over where a pigeon might or might not wander."

Ming bounded over and Jean ruffled the fur on her head playfully. "Look after him, Ming," Jean said, adding with a whisper, "Don't let the boss find him."

Tang gave a small huff before continuing to lick himself beneath his armpit.

"I told you Jean would help," Ming said, looking pleased with herself.

"She is a kind human," Francis admitted. He thought about George and wondered how he was. If he was on the front line or . . . He shook the thought away.

"You still have the capsule?" he asked.

Ming nodded.

Francis paused, wondering if he could trust Ming. He had only known her for a few hours. Real trust was something that took months to build up. Years even. But she had done more for him in a few short hours than anyone else he knew. She had all but saved his life. Besides, she was stuck in an enclosure. It wasn't like she could run away, and he didn't really have anyone else to rely on.

"Could you keep hold of it for me for a little longer? There is something I must do."

Ming watched curiously as he eased himself between two of the metal bars, being careful not to knock his damaged wing.

"Where are you going?" Ming asked, alarmed. "It's not safe to wander around the zoo in broad daylight!"

"Of course it's safe," Francis replied, gazing up at the

hazy morning sunshine. "It's a fine day to go for a stroll. If I cannot deliver this message, I need to find someone else in this zoo who can."

"But—" Ming started.

"Let him go," Tang called. "Pigeons do not belong in a zoo."

Francis smiled at Ming reassuringly. "Don't worry, I'll be back."

It certainly was a pleasant day for a stroll, Francis thought. Zookeepers bustled around, cleaning out enclosures and feeding the animals, preparing to open for the day. They paid him no mind as he strutted along. When the night drew in, though, it would be a different matter. They would huddle in their homes in the dark, afraid to set foot outside in case there was another air raid.

The giant pandas' enclosure was at the end of a long path. Francis followed the path to the center of the zoo, where a large wooden pavilion stood in a vast grassy area peppered with wooden picnic tables. He gazed up at a wooden sign on which a map of the zoo was posted. Four other paths led off from his in different directions. In the distance, Francis could see the top of a large building, and along the path to his left was a café and a wide-arched tunnel that seemed to lead out of the zoo. Behind that, tall nets hung over another row of enclosures. Francis decided to go straight and see what animals the zoo contained.

As he walked, Francis wondered how long it would be until the bombers returned. He hoped there would be at least be enough time to get his message to Bletchley. A horrible chill ran down Francis's spine. What if he was Britain's only hope? What if he was the only creature who could warn the Allies about Operation Sea Lion? He hurried on, his thoughts of the pleasant day forgotten. He had to find someone reliable to take the message for him. But he couldn't entrust just any old creature with his mission. It had to be someone brave, determined, and, above all, loyal to their country.

He reached the penguin pool, where dark black-and-white shapes glided past an underwater window, swimming elegantly to and fro. Francis could never understand why the humans considered penguins to be birds. They were more fish than bird. What was the point of having wings when you couldn't fly? He looked down at his injured wing and tried to move it. Nothing. He was as useless as a penguin.

He approached an enclosure similar to Ming's and peered through the bars for a glimpse of what was inside.

"Ahem! Excuse me?" he called. "Is there anyone in there who thinks they might have it in them to become a hero?"

In reply, a massive lion launched itself at the bars with an almighty roar. Francis jerked his head back, narrowly avoiding the beast's claws, which scraped across the bars with a screeching noise that set Francis's beak on edge.

"I'll help you," the lion growled, prowling back and forth. "Come inside and tell me more."

Francis backed away, shaking his head vigorously. "Th-that's all right," he stuttered. "I'm very sorry to have bothered you."

Francis scurried away, cursing his own stupidity. He had to think more clearly. He couldn't choose *any* animal. It had to be one that would be able to navigate its way through London unnoticed. Not a lion or elephant—they would only draw attention. Perhaps another bird? Either way, he had to make sure he didn't go near any animal that would eat him before he'd even told them about the mission.

He paused. How was he going to convince the right animal to take on the mission when he wasn't even able to *talk* about the mission?

He was lost in thought when something hit him on the back of the head. He turned but there was no one in sight. He continued on when something hit him again. It was an empty peanut shell. He caught the smallest of movements on the wall beside him.

He pretended to walk away, but then spun to face his attacker, getting hit directly in the face by another nut.

"Ouch!" Francis cried. "There was really no need for that."

He pecked at the nut on the ground and found that it was actually quite tasty.

"Sorry!" A voice giggled.

"We were only playing," said another.

Francis hopped onto the low wall so that he could see who he was talking to. Two small gray heads popped up, their wide eyes sparkling with mischief.

"Give me another one of those nuts," Francis said, "then we'll call it even."

One of the monkeys threw another nut. This time Francis caught it in his beak, and the monkeys clapped their hands together in delight. He mumbled his thanks as he crunched it up, watching the monkeys leap across a wooden platform, swinging on ropes and ducking beneath branches.

In the middle of the enclosure was a hill built with

blocks of concrete and stone, sculpted to look like a natural rock formation. A sign in front read: SQUIRREL MONKEYS.

A wall circled the enclosure, and just out of reach was an abandoned sandwich. A group of monkeys joined forces, hanging upside down in a chain until the lowest one was able to swing out enough to grab the sandwich. The monkeys chattered excitedly as they shared it between them.

"That was rather clever," Francis called. *And stealth-like*, he thought.

Two of the monkeys bounded over, grinning. "We're very resourceful when we want to be," one said. "I'm Jacky. Nice to meet you."

"Francis," Francis replied, with a small bow.

"I'm Chiney," the other added with a wink. "We're only clever when the humans aren't around. We can't let them know how clever we really are, otherwise they'd never leave us alone."

"We were at Whipsnade for a while," said Jacky. "We had a nice island, surrounded by water, with a cave in the middle where we slept and a giant monkey puzzle tree to climb. The humans thought we couldn't swim, so there was only a low wall on the other side of the moat.

"Except one day, one of us—Gerald—got a bit bored, so he decided to swim across to the other side and see what was over there. He jumped the wall and made off toward the giraffe house."

"And was never seen again," Chiney added with a sigh. "We like to think that he made a new life for himself, somewhere out there."

Francis laughed. "How did you end up here?"

"As soon as the humans found out that we could just up and leave whenever we liked, they moved us to London where they could keep us locked away." Chiney gave Francis a wicked grin. "Of course, *everyone* knows that you can't keep a monkey caged. If we wanted to leave, we could. Anytime we wanted."

"Is that so?" Francis asked, a plan forming in his mind. "Then why don't you?"

"There's nothing out there for us," Jacky said. "Besides, we like it here. We get all the food we can eat, and the humans love us. Of course, that's not to say that we don't have the odd adventure now and then."

Francis smiled. "You might be just the animals I've been looking for," he said. "I have a message to deliver. A rather important message, only I'm unable to deliver it myself because..." He held up his bandaged wing.

"Oh dear," said Jacky. "That doesn't look good."

Francis shook his head. "It isn't. But this message I have to deliver is very urgent, and I can't wait until my wing is healed to deliver it."

He glanced sideways at the monkeys. "I've been trying to think of a way to get the message to where it needs to go. Maybe even find someone who might be brave and smart enough to take on the challenge, but..." He sighed again, watching as Chiney whispered something into Jacky's ear.

"We'll do it!" Chiney said, but Jacky shook his head.

"What's in it for us?" he asked. "It's risky breaking out of the zoo. We might get caught, and then who knows what will happen to us."

Chiney opened his mouth to interject, but Jacky held a paw up.

"Good question," Francis said. "Of course, you need to know exactly what the mission...plan...involves. It's quite simple. All we need to do is find a map so that I can show you where you need to go, and then give you the message to take to the humans."

"Humans?" Jacky cried. "See?" He turned to Chiney. "I'm not getting into anything that involves humans."

"Wait, wait!" Francis begged. He sighed. Jacky was right—the plan involved a lot of risk. Francis owed them the truth so that they knew what they were getting themselves into.

He took a deep breath. "I am a member of the National Pigeon Service. I work with the humans to deliver messages of the utmost importance to a codebreaking facility so that we can stay ahead of the enemy and defeat them. The message I need to deliver could change the entire outcome of the war in our favor."

Jacky and Chiney stared at Francis, their mouths hanging open and their eyes wide, then they burst out laughing.

Francis waited impatiently until they had calmed down.

Jacky saw the look on his face and gave a nervous laugh, then shut his mouth. "Are you being serious?" he asked. "You want us to help you on a real mission?"

"We could be heroes!" Chiney gushed.

"Yes, well, I suppose you would be heroes in a way," Francis said.

"Well, why didn't you say that to begin with?" Jacky asked. "Count us in!"

CHAPTER 6
MING

September 11, 1940

Over the next few nights, more bombs came. The planes flew over as soon as the sun had set, their silhouettes creating monstrous shapes across the purple sky. The sounds of bombs and gunfire continued all night and into the morning, only disappearing when the sun rose.

Ming's nerves were in tatters. There was no chance of getting any rest through the night, so she slept while she could during the day. Jean tried to prompt Ming and Tang to move out of the back of the enclosure and show themselves to the ever-dwindling crowds, but Ming just didn't have it in her to come out of her hiding place, so eventually Jean let them be.

Francis had hidden his secret message capsule beneath the straw they slept on, and he sat upon it like a protective hen and her chick. Jean pretended that she didn't know Francis was there, but she always left a handful of seeds along with the pandas' bamboo.

The sound of heavy gunfire from the planes echoed around the zoo. Ming scooted closer to Francis, being mindful of his wing. Tang somehow slept through the whole thing. He had gotten used to it, he'd said in a bored voice, and wasn't going to waste any more time worrying about whether he would live or die each night.

Francis peeped one eye open and glanced at Ming. "Can't sleep?" he asked.

Ming shook her head, hiding her shaking paws in her lap.

"Was it true…what Tang said?" he asked. "That you didn't really speak until you met me?"

Ming opened her mouth to answer, then closed it again with a sigh. It was so hard to explain. When the humans had brought her to a strange, new land, she had been so scared and bewildered that she had lost her voice. By the time Tang came along, she'd been so used to keeping quiet, she'd almost forgotten how to talk out loud.

But there was part of her that thought that maybe she didn't *want* to talk. Or to connect with Tang. It felt easier that way. Because what happened if she started to talk about her family and her home and she could never stop? What if it brought all that pain back again? What if she began to care about Tang and he, too, was taken away from her? Instead, she buried it deep down inside where it couldn't hurt her.

"I think I may have found a solution to my problem," Francis said, seeming to sense Ming's discomfort and changing the subject. He gestured at the red capsule. "I just need to check on a few things first."

He stood stiffly and took off toward the bars. The farther he walked, the faster Ming's heart raced. The noise of the planes in the sky and the flashes of explosions merged into a cacophony of chaos inside her head.

"Wait!" Ming called. "Will you stay, please?"

Francis paused, then came back to perch beside her as more planes flew overhead.

"Those are Spitfires," Francis told her. "They belong to us, the British. You see the rings and circles on the side and beneath the wings?" Ming nodded. "That's how you know they are friendly. Whenever you see them in the sky there's no need to worry; they will soon chase the enemy away."

"What about the enemy planes, though?" Ming asked, a quaver in her voice. "How do I spot those?"

"They have black-and-white crosses on them," Francis said. "But the Spitfires will chase them away before they get too close."

Ming sat in silence for a while, unconvinced.

"It's all right to be afraid, you know," he said. "I've recently spent time in the middle of a war zone, where the noise and the fighting and the..." He paused, lifting his wing at the sky. "It was much worse than this. The humans trained me to fly through the harshest weather, to cope with the loudest noises and the most terrible distractions, but it didn't ever stop me from being afraid."

"How did you get through it?" Ming asked.

Francis sighed. "At some point you have to decide what is more important: your fear or your mission. Don't let fear stop you from doing what you want to do. What you *need* to do."

Ming lifted the red capsule between her paws delicately, as though it was the most precious object in the world. Which to Francis, she supposed, it was. "This is really important to you, isn't it?"

"This invasion is only the beginning," Francis said. "The Nazis are testing our resolve. Trying to make us lose faith, using our fears against us. When they think there is no more fight left in us, they are planning to do something much worse."

Ming's stomach lurched. "What could be worse than this?" she whispered.

"That's something I hope we will never have to find out," Francis said.

"Where do you need to deliver your message to?" she asked.

Francis glanced around. "There is a special facility," he whispered. "At Bletchley Park, outside of London. I was heading there when I was shot down. It is where I was born and trained to be part of the National Pigeon Service. I must get this message to the code breakers there to warn them about the enemy's plans."

Ming's thoughts raced. Maybe it was because Francis understood the ways of the humans and their war, or maybe it was his bravery that comforted her, but she wanted him to stay with her. Still, she knew deep down that those thoughts were selfish. Francis's mission was far greater than her needs. She took a deep breath and summoned the words she knew she had to say:

"You should go," Ming said.

Francis gave her a puzzled look. "But my wing isn't healed."

She shook her head. "Not to Bletchley—you should go and find a way to deliver your message."

"Are you sure?" Francis asked. "I'll be as quick as I can. You'll hardly miss me."

"This war has brought nothing but misery," Ming said. "Our food has been rationed and we get less and less each day. And it's no better for the humans. They have to run and hide each time the sirens sound, and sometimes..." She paused. "Sometimes some of the zookeepers have gone away. But if there's a way your message can stop some of this misery, then you must do what you can. There is no time to waste."

CHAPTER 7
FRANCIS

September 13, 1940

Two days later, Francis was rudely awoken from his afternoon nap as the enclosure door clanged open. The plan had been put into action—the monkeys were going to find out where they could procure a map. They already knew how to get themselves in and out of their cage unnoticed. Despite his impatience, all Francis could do was wait.

He quickly buried himself beneath the straw as Jean appeared. She reminded Francis of George in many ways. He stayed as quiet as he could in case she wasn't alone.

He was right to be cautious. The boss barged his way past Jean and began flinging up discarded bamboo and straw, searching feverishly for something. Francis had more than a sneaking suspicion that that *something* was a pigeon. He peered out through the straw. The man seemed almost desperate. *What if he is a spy?* Francis thought suddenly. Maybe he had been sent by the Nazis to retrieve the capsule! Francis checked that the capsule was well hidden but, to his horror, found that it was gone.

"He's not here!" Jean protested, glancing nervously at the giant pandas. "I released him in the park, just like you told me to."

The boss ignored her and crawled beneath the wooden platform. "There have been reports of a pigeon with a bandaged wing strutting around the zoo, distracting the visitors," the man's voice echoed.

Francis frantically hunted through the straw and dirt for the capsule. It had been there only moments ago. Where could it have possibly gone?

"What's the matter?" Ming mumbled, her eyes never leaving the crazed man.

"The capsule!" Francis hissed. "It's gone."

Ming's eyes widened and she swept her paws back and forth through the straw around her, searching for the capsule.

"Psst!"

Tang gestured to his paw. He checked that the boss

was still beneath the platform, then slowly opened his paw slightly, revealing a glimpse of red.

The capsule.

"Tang!" Ming chided.

Francis breathed in relief, ducking behind Ming just as the boss emerged from the platform, bottom first. He stood and brushed down his trousers, then ran his fingers through his thinning hair, covering himself in a sticky, brown substance.

Francis tried not to laugh as he realized what was streaked through the man's hair, while Ming began shaking.

"Are you all right?" Francis whispered.

Tang was doing the same thing, and Francis realized that they were laughing. Ming couldn't control herself any longer—a loud hooting roar burst from her mouth. She fell sideways, laughing and clutching at her stomach.

Francis couldn't help but smile. Until he noticed Jean staring at him, her face white. And she wasn't the only one who could see him. The boss watched him, too. Except his expression was not one of horror, like Jean's. It was one of pure triumph.

"I knew it!" the man snapped, jolting Ming and Tang from their hysterics.

"H-he must have found his way back," Jean stuttered. "I didn't know he was here, sir. I can't control what a pigeon does."

The boss made a noise that sounded like a low growl. Francis felt a twist in his gut. He strode toward Francis, reaching him in a few long steps. Francis backed up, but his tail feathers hit the wall. He was cornered.

"Please, sir," Jean begged. "I'll take him farther away this time so that he can't return."

She put her hand on his arm, but he shook her off, focused only on Francis.

The two looked at each other for a moment, the man's eyes full of inexplicable hatred, and Francis's full of fear. At least the message was safe, he thought. Maybe, if he made it out of this, he could return later to retrieve it.

Francis closed his eyes as the man moved toward him, when suddenly a growl issued from behind him. Francis opened his eyes again. Ming and Tang stood on either side of the boss, their stares intense, warning the man to not move any closer.

"Stay away from our friend," Tang growled.

"I think the pandas quite like the pigeon," Jean said quietly.

"Make them back away!" the boss ordered.

Jean shook her head. "I can't, *sir*. They are not performing monkeys."

The man scowled and tried to grab Francis, but Ming and Tang growled again. The noise sent a shiver of fear through Francis, even though he knew they would never hurt him.

"Giant pandas can become very protective of their young," Jean continued. "Perhaps they see this pigeon as one of their own. It wouldn't be wise to upset them."

"They belong to *me*," the boss retorted. "And they will do what I tell them to do. Stand down!" he shouted at the pandas.

But the pandas didn't stand down. They moved in, backing the man into a corner, just as he'd done to Francis. Filthy trails of sweat slid down the man's face, leaving behind streaks of brown from the dung in his hair. He stomped his feet in frustration.

A siren pierced the silence, and Francis almost jumped out of his skin.

"Air raid!" the man shouted, seizing his chance to make a hasty escape. "Quickly, Jean!"

Jean smiled briefly at Francis before leaving, slamming the door shut behind her with an echoing clang.

"That was close," Francis breathed. "He must have

been after the capsule. Enemy spies are everywhere. Thank goodness you hid it, Tang."

Tang smiled proudly.

"What are we going to do now?" Ming asked. "He's sure to come back for you."

Francis sighed. "I'll have to move up my plans to ensure that he can't get his hands on the message."

"But what about you?" Tang asked.

Francis raised his bandaged wing. "I can't get very far. We will have to remain extra vigilant so that dreadful man doesn't find me again."

He looked at their worried faces. "It's all right," he told them. "Every pigeon in the service knows that when they are sent out on a mission, there is a high chance that they won't make it back alive. But that's a risk I am prepared to take for my country."

He squinted at a sliver of light coming from behind Ming. He hopped closer to the door. It was slightly ajar. In her haste, Jean must have forgotten to lock the door.

Francis turned back to Ming. "How would you like to help me?" he asked.

Ming gave him a quizzical look, and Francis gestured

his good wing at the open door. "Come and meet some very clever friends of mine."

"You *can't!*" Tang chided as Ming moved forward. "You'll be caught in an instant, and we'll *both* be punished. Besides, there's an air raid going on, remember?"

Francis looked up to the sky. The sirens were still blaring but there weren't any planes in the sky yet, and the few rounds of gunfire that he could hear sounded miles away.

"You'll be safe with me," Francis told Ming.

"Go out there?" Ming squeaked. "Without a human?"

"What do you need a human for?" Francis asked. "You are your own animal with your own head and your own heart. How often do you get a chance to be free?"

"Tang?" Ming asked. "Are you coming?"

Tang hesitated. "I'll stay here. In case the boss comes back. But don't be too long."

Ming took a deep breath and smiled a real smile for the first time since Francis had arrived. "All right," she said. "I'll do it."

September 13, 1940

Ming couldn't believe that she was walking around the zoo in broad daylight, with not a human in sight. It was terrifying and exhilarating all at once. The most daring thing she'd ever done in her life up until now was talking to Francis when he'd landed in her enclosure. But despite the fear squirming in her belly, she was going to do what *she* wanted for once.

When she was a cub, she'd sometimes been allowed to wander free—supervised by a human, of course— while children and adults alike gathered around her, oohing and aahing at her precocious clumsiness.

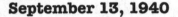

A little way ahead, a pair of llamas lazily munched on

a patch of grass beside a large pavilion. Both llamas had thick, curly fur, one white and one light brown. Their backs were laden with sacks and blankets as though they were about to go off on a mountain expedition.

"What are you two doing?" Ming asked the llamas, who had paused to watch the unusual sight of a panda and pigeon.

"We could ask you the same thing," the white llama replied.

"We're on an adventure, aren't we, Ming?"

The idea was so absurd that Ming could only grin in reply.

"Lucky for some," the other llama replied dryly. "We were taking supplies to the giraffes' enclosure when the sirens started. The humans didn't even give us a backward glance as they ran for shelter. We thought we'd make the most of our free time until they put us back to work again."

"They are making you work?" Ming asked incredulously. "But why?"

The light brown llama sniffed, then nodded to a building behind them where a motor vehicle was parked. "They can't use their machines anymore," he said. "Not since the war started. The fuel they need is rationed, and it only lasts a short while before it runs out."

"So they have to use us instead," said the white llama.

"That seems a bit unfair," Francis said.

"It's not so bad. It gets us out of our paddock and we get to visit our friends around the zoo. Besides, we're not the only ones. The camels have been carrying the bigger sacks of food around the zoo. Even the Shetland ponies carry fodder on smaller journeys. It's a war. Everyone has to do their part so that we all survive."

"Very true," Francis said sternly. "I applaud your work ethic. I myself have a very important mission to undertake to ensure the safety of our great country."

The white llama snorted, sending a spray of spittle into Ming's face. She grimaced and wiped it away with a paw.

"You?" he guffawed. "What can a pigeon do for the war effort?"

Francis's feathers ruffled indignantly.

"Let's have a look over here," Ming interjected, nudging Francis with her nose. "I've always wanted to see the polar bears. Tang thinks that they are just like us, minus a color."

Francis stalked off in the direction of the polar bears. Theirs was a large, open enclosure with rocky terraces built within. A low wall studded with jagged rock sat at the front to keep the humans out and the polar bears in. But there were no polar bears to be seen.

"Where are they?" Ming wondered out loud.

"Maybe they were evacuated to Whipsnade?" Francis suggested.

Ming frowned. "Maybe, but I didn't see them when we were there," she said. She wandered around to the side of the enclosure. "Can you hear that?"

It was very faint, but she thought she heard a keening sound, a bit like the noise Tang sometimes made in his sleep when he was having a bad dream. Francis hopped ahead.

"It looks like some kind of tunnel," he said. There was a large reinforced metal door covering the entranceway, and as Ming placed her ear against it she could clearly hear the sounds of large animals inside.

"It's to keep them safe." A squawk came from above.

Ming lifted her head to see a large blackbird perched in the tree.

"Keep who safe?" she asked. "The polar bears?"

She wondered why she and Tang didn't have somewhere safe to go when the sirens sounded. Why were polar bears more important than pandas?

The blackbird chittered. "Of course not the polar bears! The *humans*. In case the zoo is bombed and they escape. Have you ever seen a polar bear?" He looked Ming up and down. "You look a bit like one actually, but a bit more round and fluffy."

"I am neither round nor fluffy!" Ming huffed.

"You are a little bit," Francis mumbled beside her. "Have you seen the little Ming toys? They are absolutely adorable!"

Ming gave him a sharp look and he snapped his beak shut.

"Anyway," the blackbird continued, "if you had ever seen a polar bear, you would know how deadly they are. Sometimes I hang around here at feeding time, and it's a bloodbath! The way they use their sharp teeth to rip into the..."

Ming felt her breakfast rise in her throat.

"I think that's quite enough," Francis said, seeing the look on her face.

"Maybe I'm not related to polar bears after all," Ming mumbled. "Makes me glad I'm a vegetarian."

"Me too," Francis said. "Otherwise I would have been a goner when I landed in your enclosure. Come on. Let's see if my new friends have made good progress with phase one of our plan."

He led her to the monkey enclosure, and they were immediately greeted by loud whoops from two little monkeys. They leaped through the branches to where Francis stood outside their cage. Their heads and faces were gray, and their huge eyes twinkled with mischief as they performed tricks. Ming could see why Francis liked them so much.

When they had finished their show of twirls and cartwheels and death-defying leaps through the air, Ming stamped her paws on the ground in appreciation. The monkeys jumped down to grin at her through the other side of the wire fence.

"Madam," said one of the monkeys, giving her a low bow. "Welcome to Monkey Hill."

"Nice to see you, Francis," the other said.

"Ming, this is Chiney and Jacky."

Ming gave them a shy smile.

"Have you made any headway with the map?" Francis asked anxiously.

"We have. The camels told the llamas, who told the

Shetland ponies, who told us that there's a large map in the administration building," Chiney told them.

"There's one problem, though," Jacky said with a frown. "It's in the boss's office."

"We had the pleasure of his company earlier," Ming said with a shudder.

Francis's eyes brightened. "We could do it the next time the sirens sound! The humans will be in the shelters so it will be easy."

Ming's stomach lurched. "Not if there is an attack on the zoo," she said. "Have you really thought this through?"

Francis nodded, then looked at the monkeys to see what their response would be. Chiney grinned and gave a thumbs-up. Jacky sighed, then nodded, too.

"So you'll do it?" Francis asked. "You'll deliver my message?"

"We're in," Jacky said. "We're tired of this war. The little monkeys are terrified. If there's something we can do to stop it, we will do it."

"Plus, it's been a while since we've caused any mischief!" Chiney added.

"Bravo!" Francis flapped his good wing in excitement. Ming tried to summon up a smile, but she didn't

feel their joy. Not when their lives could be in danger. Her blood went cold as she suddenly realized something.

"Shhh!" she hissed, quieting their celebrations. "Listen!"

Francis cocked his head to one side. "I don't hear anything."

"Exactly!" Ming cried. "The sirens have stopped. That means that the—"

"Humans!" screamed the monkeys, jumping up and down as the keepers and workers returned to their posts.

"The boss!" Ming cried. "He'll be coming straight back to my enclosure. We have to get back there!"

Francis's head swept from side to side. "There's no way back without being spotted."

Chiney winked at Ming. "You head back to your enclosure. We'll take care of the rest."

"Go!" Jacky shouted.

Ming didn't wait to be told twice. She hurried away with Francis struggling to keep up. Ming raced on, expecting to be caught at any moment. Instead, a sudden loud shriek rang out behind her, followed by laughter and applause. She paused to glance back. The monkeys had escaped their enclosure and were running riot among the gathering crowd of zookeepers. They were mostly women, like Jean, volunteers who had stepped in after the men left their jobs to go to war. The monkeys pulled hats off the keepers' heads and raided the cotton candy stall. A couple of the monkeys, she noticed, had intercepted the boss and were pulling vigorously at the bottom of his trouser legs.

Francis hid behind a trash can outside the enclosure, while Ming squeezed back inside. Tang slid the door shut and they both slumped to the floor, trying to look as calm as possible.

A second later, Jean arrived.

CHAPTER 9

FRANCIS

September 19, 1940

After they'd almost been caught, Francis kept a low profile. Luckily, Jean seemed to be on Francis's side. She was a good sort, Francis thought. If there had been a way to communicate with her, he would have considered asking her to deliver the message. Francis was more and more convinced, however, that the boss was an enemy spy.

He thought about George again. George would have liked Jean. George was a gentle sort just like her; he wasn't made for fighting, he was made for caring for animals.

Francis's plans had been delayed and he was becoming more and more frantic by the hour. There hadn't yet been an air raid for them to put their plan in action. They still needed to break into the boss's office. The camels had told Francis that they'd spied a large map of Britain through the boss's window when they were delivering supplies. Once Francis and the monkeys had procured the map, they'd leave for Bletchley immediately. Francis wished he could accompany them to Bletchley, but speed was vital and he would slow their progress. At least he could help get the map, though.

Francis had split the plan into two parts. Part one: get the map. Part two (as long as they weren't caught): the monkeys would escape in the dead of night to deliver the message. By the time the humans discovered that the monkeys were missing, Jacky and Chiney would be far out of the city.

Hopefully.

The monkeys were cunning enough that they should be able to make their way unnoticed.

"I haven't seen the boss today," Tang remarked. "Maybe you could get the map now?"

"It's too risky," Ming said. "Too many humans around."

Francis stomped his feet in frustration. "The longer

we wait, the less chance there is of the message getting through to the right people. Once the Nazis launch their attack, it will be too late. I have to get that map tonight," he said.

Francis could hardly breathe. He felt as though a huge weight was pressing down upon his chest.

Ming smiled at him and he felt the pressure ease a little. "You can do it," she said. "If anyone can, it's you."

"She's right," Tang said. "You're pretty remarkable. For a pigeon."

Ming gasped. "Did you say that I am *right*?" she teased. "Did you hear that, Francis? Tang agreed with me for once!"

Francis forced out a laugh, but his mind was racing. He was grateful for their confidence in him, but he felt more and more unsure of himself, as though he were forgetting his place in the world.

He waited impatiently as the zoo shut down for the day and a hush fell upon them. After the recent air raids, the silence felt oddly wrong. Ming and Tang mouthed "Good luck" at Francis as he hopped between the bars. He gave them a small wave with his good wing and headed to Monkey Hill.

Jacky and Chiney were already waiting outside the monkey enclosure. They scurried over to him.

"We're out of time," Francis said. "We have to raid the boss's office tonight, sirens or no sirens. Are you ready?"

Chiney grinned. "We were born ready!"

"Do you know the way?" Francis asked, worried that they might have missed a vital point in their plan.

Chiney pointed at a large wooden noticeboard. A color map of the zoo had been pinned to it, with the buildings numbered and labeled, and a key down one side. The administration office was labeled in bright red. Francis studied the map, checking and double-checking the route until he was certain that he knew where he was going.

Jacky glanced around nervously. "Keep an eye out for humans."

The monkeys led the way to the main offices on the other side of the zoo. Francis stared in horror at the caged birds as they passed a giant aviary. He paused, watching as they flew back and forth beneath the raised netting covering their cage.

"*Where are you going?*" the small birds chittered.

"*What are you doing?*" Francis ignored them. There was no time for small talk.

The birds were beautiful, their feathers so brightly colored that they made Francis feel dull in contrast. The thought of not being able to fly for any distance, *ever*, scared Francis more than any war could. One of the birds was hidden in the shadows, and Francis suddenly felt guilty for ever complaining about being a pigeon. He gave the bird a small smile, but the bird just stared back, emotionless.

They continued on, past the camel house and across the lawn where he and Ming had met the llamas. Past a restaurant, and then finally they reached the tunnel entrance at the very edge of the zoo.

"The east tunnel," Jacky said.

"This leads into Regent's Park," Francis said, remembering the map. "The main office is across the road on the other side."

They crept through the dark tunnel, their footsteps echoing within the stone walls. At the end, Francis peeped out cautiously. Although it was dark and there was a curfew, a few humans still wandered along the road. Francis could hear the sounds of motor cars in the distance. As soon as he was sure that the coast was clear, he gestured to the monkeys to follow, then half ran, half jumped across the road until he was safely across.

"This is it," Chiney said, looking up at the redbrick building in front of them.

"Let's hope they have what we're looking for," Francis said. "The next part comes down to you."

The monkeys scaled a black drainpipe running down one side of the building until they came to a window on the first floor. "I think this is the boss's office," Chiney called down to Francis.

Chiney climbed over Jacky's back and took hold of the windowsill. Francis held his breath as Jacky swung from the drainpipe, performing an impressive backflip up and over Chiney to land feetfirst on the narrow window ledge. Jacky joined him, and the two monkeys seemed to argue for a moment.

"There's no way in!" Jacky called down to Francis.

Francis surveyed the building. The windows were closed and the door was secure. He started to think that their plan had failed at the first hurdle, when he heard a flutter of wings above and a cooing sound. A moment later, a pigeon took off from the roof.

"Of course!" Francis cried. "The chimney!" he told Jacky. "Can you fit down the chimney?"

Jacky gave Francis a nod, and he and Chiney clambered farther up the drainpipe, along the gutters, and up onto the roof tiles until they were out of sight.

Francis held his breath hoping that the monkeys wouldn't get stuck, or caught, when he heard the lock at the front door being slid open. The monkeys appeared in the open doorway, their fur slightly soot-covered, and bowed dramatically.

"Welcome to our humble abode," Chiney joked.

Francis hurried inside and the three of them entered the closest room. It looked like an office. At either end of the room were two large oak desks, covered with papers and files. Francis took a look at one while the monkeys checked out the other, riffling through papers and throwing them in the air when they were not what they were looking for.

"Don't make a mess!" Francis hissed. "We don't want anyone to know we were here, in case they guess what we we're looking for."

Chiney frowned at Francis uncertainly, but he took more care to keep the papers in order.

"I don't think it's in here," Jacky said. "The camels mentioned it being on a wall."

"That's it!" Chiney said. "We need to find a room where the camels could spy through the window."

They moved along the darkened hallway to a room at the back of the house. Francis nudged the door open slightly with his head, and the door gave a loud creak. They froze, waiting to see if anyone was still in the building who might have heard them. When no one came, they ventured into the room.

"It's there!" Chiney cried, pointing to the wall.

Jacky slapped a paw over his mouth and gestured wide-eyed to Francis with his tail. Two large armchairs sat in front of a fireplace. One was empty, but a loud snort and grumble came from the other chair. Francis moved as quietly as he could and saw two large feet set on the floor, attached to two legs wearing gray pajamas, which led to a human asleep in the armchair, his mouth open wide as he snored loudly.

"*The boss!*" Francis hissed.

Jacky gestured at the door, suggesting that they should leave. Francis looked at the boss, then at the map on the wall. It was so close, he couldn't bear it. If they left now, empty-handed, they might not get another opportunity to return. But if they stayed, and the boss found Francis in his office with the monkeys…Francis gulped.

He looked at his new friends and realized that he couldn't put them in danger.

"Go!" Francis whispered. "I'll get the map."

Jacky shook his head. "We said we'd help you and we will," he whispered back.

Francis hopped up onto a chair, then onto the desk. He pulled at the lower corners of the map with his beak, trying to ease it away from the wall without ripping it or alerting the boss to their presence.

Jacky pulled at one top corner, while Chiney took the other. Slowly, slowly, the map began to peel away from the wall. It was almost free when Francis lost his balance, knocking into a pot of ink. The inkpot wobbled back and forth for a few terrifying seconds. Then, impossibly slowly, it fell onto its side and began rolling across the desk. Francis leaped forward, reaching his beak toward it to stop it from smashing to the floor. As his beak grazed the pot, it fell over the edge of the desk. Time seemed to stand still as Francis could do nothing but watch it drop. Then, at the last second, Jacky's tail swooped in and grasped the inkpot.

The three stared at one another, none of them daring to breathe or make a sound. Francis slowly turned to look at the boss. His feet remained motionless. The monkeys helped to roll up the map, then they made their way silently across the floor, hurried out the door, and rushed down the stairs as fast as they could, not stopping until they were in the relative safety of the tunnel.

"That was close!" Francis gasped.

He looked at Jacky and Chiney, who were breathing fast, and laughed. "We did it!" he said. "We actually did it. Right under the boss's nose as well." He gestured to the map. "Let's take a look."

Jacky placed the map onto the ground and Francis used his beak to open it up to its full size. He scoured the name places until he found what he was searching for.

"That's it!" he said excitedly, tapping his beak to where Bletchley Park was located. "This is where you need to go."

The monkeys leaned over his shoulder. "That's where we are," Jacky said, pointing to Regent's Park.

"It's farther than I thought," Chiney said, all of his

earlier excitement about the mission gone. "What if we get caught? If the boss had woken up in there..." He didn't finish his sentence. He didn't need to.

Francis examined the map again. It did seem rather a long way. He could cover a lot more ground when he was flying. The monkeys would have to make the journey by foot, and who knew what obstacles they might encounter on the way? Francis's stomach dropped. He couldn't let them take such a risk on his behalf.

"We'll do it," Jacky said.

"Are you sure?" Francis asked.

Chiney took a deep breath, then nodded. "You promised an adventure, and this journey will certainly be that."

"You can change your mind," Francis said. "I can find another way."

"We'll do it," Jacky repeated. "We know what is at stake if we go, but we also know what might be at stake if we don't. We want to help, Francis. We don't want to be stuck in this human war anymore."

"All right," Francis said. "If you are absolutely certain. Go back to Monkey Hill and study the map—it will be better if you know it by heart rather than taking it with you. Tomorrow, we put the second part of the plan into action."

"We'll go on ahead," Jacky said. "We should make sure we're not seen together."

Francis watched them disappear into the darkness, when suddenly there was a flash of lights and the pounding of footsteps along the pavement. Francis raced around the corner to see the monkeys being held by two men in uniform. Jacky dropped the map and it rolled beneath a bush as he continued to struggle free. The monkeys did their best to escape, wriggling and waving their arms around, but it was no good.

They had been caught before they'd even left the zoo.

CHAPTER 10
FRANCIS

September 19, 1940

The soldiers pounded on the door of the administration office Francis and the monkeys had just left. A light came on in a window at the very top, and Francis hurried to the bush to retrieve the map. He gasped as Jean appeared in the doorway, relief flooding through him. He hadn't realized that Jean lived so close to the zoo. Jean's eyes widened as she saw the escapees. Francis couldn't hear what she was saying, but she called out behind her, then disappeared into the building.

A dark shadow filled the doorway, and Francis's hopes vanished. It was the boss.

The boss scowled at the monkeys and held up a small

cage. The soldiers helped him to usher the monkeys inside, which was no easy feat. They twisted and wriggled. Jacky almost made it out of the cage at one point, but the boss slammed the door shut in the monkey's face.

Francis's heart sank as his friends were forced to accept defeat. He stomped his feet on the ground in anger, at the boss, the interfering soldiers, and himself. This was all his fault. He shouldn't have encouraged the monkeys to go through with the plan. They should be safely on Monkey Hill with the rest of their family, playing and swinging without a care in the world.

Who knew what the boss might do with them now. Francis hoped that Jean would ensure they came to no harm, but he already knew that she had little influence over the boss.

The boss set off at full speed, carrying the monkeys back toward their enclosure. Francis followed, keeping to the shadows with the map held tightly in his beak. The boss reached Monkey Hill and disappeared around to the enclosure's back entrance. Francis debated whether to go after them or remain where he was. His instincts told him to wait.

A few heart-pounding moments later, the boss

emerged. He wrapped his patterned bathrobe tightly around himself and stalked off into the night. When the coast was clear, Francis approached the monkeys' enclosure. "Chiney?" he whispered. "Jacky? Are you all right?"

There was a horrible silence. Francis became aware that he couldn't see any monkeys. Usually they slept on top of the crags and ledges of Monkey Hill, but it was deserted.

Suddenly, a voice rang out. "Over here!" Jacky shouted.

"Where is Chiney?" Francis asked. "And the other monkeys?"

"They're right here," Chiney replied, swinging through the air to land beside Jacky.

Francis looked up at Monkey Hill as heads and tails appeared from beneath the crags and ledges.

"They were hiding?"

Chiney nodded. "They thought they might be in trouble."

Francis's head drooped. "I'm so sorry," he whispered. "I didn't mean for you to get caught."

"It was our fault," Jacky said. "We forgot about

the soldiers. They are staying at a house on the edge of Regent's Park until they are called up for service. They sometimes patrol at night."

"Do you have the map?" Jacky asked. "I dropped it when the soldier grabbed me."

Francis nodded. "What are you going to do now?" Chiney asked.

Francis sighed. "I'll have to find another way," he said.

He bid the monkeys a sad farewell and took the longer route back to the giant pandas' enclosure. He couldn't bear to see the disappointment in Ming's face. What was he going to tell her? That there was no hope of getting the message to Bletchley in time for it to make a difference?

He moved his bad wing slightly up and down, testing it to see if it might be healed enough for him to fly. It felt stiff but not too painful. He moved it higher, then faster, then...

"Argghh!" he cried out as a bolt of red-hot pain shot through his wing. He lowered it in defeat, holding it close to his body. He wouldn't be flying anywhere soon.

There was a high-pitched trilling noise from the giant aviary. Francis froze, afraid that the boss had returned.

He might not want to hurt the zoo animals, but he wouldn't think twice about disposing of a pigeon.

"Up here," a voice trilled.

A beautiful bird, almost twice his size, peered out from behind the mesh covering her enclosure. Francis hopped closer, staring through the mesh in awe. It was the same bird that had watched him earlier.

"What *are* you?" he whispered.

"Toca," she replied, ruffling her feathers proudly. "A toucan."

She was unlike any bird Francis had ever seen, with black feathers as dark as night and a bright yellow chest. Her beak was a vivid orangey-red, as thick as a banana and curved with a black patch on the very end. Francis thought that with a beak like that she could likely scoop up an entire bag full of seed in one go.

"You're...beautiful," Francis said, feeling his face warm.

The toucan smiled back shyly, fluttering her wings. "I hope you don't mind," Toca said. "But I overheard your conversation with the monkeys. I'd like to offer my help."

Francis frowned at this. How much had she heard?

And what did she know about the mission or the dangers it held? "Help with what?" he asked innocently. "My friends and I were just out for an evening stroll."

The toucan cocked her head and narrowed her eyes at him. "I am more than just a beautiful bird, you know. I am no fool."

"I wasn't suggesting you were," Francis stuttered.

"Maybe," she said slowly, "we could help each other out? Your plan was never going to be successful with monkeys. As cunning as they are, they don't have the wing power to get very far."

She raised her wings up and down, as if to prove her point.

Francis couldn't think straight. It would certainly solve all of his problems. With her wingspan, Toca could likely fly to Bletchley and back within a few hours. But…why would she offer to do this so readily? What was in it for her?

"What is it that you want in return?" Francis asked out loud. "What do you know of my plan?"

"You've been here long enough to know that animals gossip," she said. "There has been talk of little else but the war pigeon and his heroic quest to deliver a message.

As for the *why*, I could lie to you and say that I care about the humans' war," she said. "But all I really want is to be free. To spread my wings and soar across the sky again. You understand that, don't you? I haven't been able to fly more than a few feet in so very long."

Francis could indeed understand. These last few days being confined to the ground had been almost unbearable. He couldn't imagine what it must feel like to know that you would never have the chance to fly again...to really fly...to soar across the land and sea without a care in the world, and go wherever the wind took you.

But he didn't know this bird or if he could trust her or her motives. He only had one capsule, one message, and one chance at making sure it got to Bletchley. As desperate as he was, he had to use his head and remember his training.

"All right," he said finally. "But we need to make sure we are better prepared so that this time, nothing can go wrong."

CHAPTER 11
MING

September 19, 1940

Ming paced back and forth in front of her bars, waiting for Francis. She paused every time she heard the faintest noise or saw the tiniest movement.

"Where is he?" she muttered under her breath.

"Maybe he left the zoo?" Tang suggested.

The weather that day had been hotter than the last few weeks, and the night brought little relief from the humid air. Tang sprawled out on the concrete floor, trying to cool down.

"Francis wouldn't leave without saying goodbye," Ming snapped. "Besides, he left the capsule with us. He would never leave that behind."

She continued pacing. What if Tang was right? What if Francis had decided to give up on his mission? To leave her and the message behind. It had certainly caused him no end of problems. She shook her head at herself. There was nothing more important to Francis than his mission.

She froze as another thought entered her mind. What if they had been caught, or injured? What if Francis needed Ming's help?

She glanced at Tang and made a decision. She couldn't wait around any longer.

She swiftly turned and ran at the metal door at full speed. She slammed into it hard, but barely made a dent. She staggered back as her head throbbed and her ears rang with a strange vibrating noise.

"What on earth are you doing?" Tang and Francis cried at the same time.

Ming spun around quickly—too quickly—to see multiple Francises standing in front of her. They swayed to and fro as though they were on a swing.

"Francis?" Ming squinted, trying to see straight.

"Francis is back!" Tang laughed.

Francis hopped through the bars. "Are you all right? I think half the zoo heard you crash into that door."

Ming felt her face grow hot beneath her fur. She'd been so worried about Francis that she'd gone and given herself a minor head injury.

"I'm fine," she said quickly, not wanting to dwell on her foolishness. "You were gone for so long that I thought—"

"She thought you had abandoned us," Tang interrupted dramatically, rolling himself onto his back with a groan. "It's so hot. Why don't they give us a pool? The penguins have a pool. The sea lions have a pool. Even the monkeys have a pond to splash in." He pulled at the thick fur covering his belly. "We're not made for these kind of temperatures!"

Ming ignored him.

Francis cocked his head at her. "You thought I would leave without saying goodbye?"

Ming lifted a shoulder. "Maybe," she said. "What happened?"

Francis's expression darkened. He told Ming and Tang about the monkeys being captured and the boss bringing them back to the zoo.

"At least I know that the boss is a spy for the enemy and—" He gasped suddenly. "What if Jean's in on it, too?"

He seemed to think for a moment and then shook his head. "No, of course that doesn't make sense. She could have already stolen the message. But the boss...there's something I don't trust about him. Why would he work in a zoo if he hates animals? He's obviously a Nazi spy."

"A Nazi spy?" Ming repeated, wondering if she wasn't the only one with a head injury.

"But..." Francis continued, seeming to have lost his mind. "Jean was with him. Maybe she is in on it, or he's been fooling her this entire time?"

Tang gaped at Francis. "In on what?" he asked, looking at Ming.

"Francis," Ming said gently, "Jean *helped* you. She is good and kind. You know that. And as for the boss, he's not the most pleasant of humans, but I'm sure he isn't a spy."

"You don't know that for sure," Francis spluttered.

"He can't be all bad if Jean is his daughter," Ming continued.

"There's no explanation for it," Francis said. "Wait— did you say she's his daughter?"

Tang nodded slowly.

Francis made a face. "But she's so...and he's so... and why does she call him 'sir' if he's her father?"

"When the war started, many of the male keepers were sent away to join the fighting forces," Ming said. "The boss only remained because he is too old to be enlisted, and so the other keepers were replaced by volunteers—mostly women—and Jean was one of them."

"Oh," Francis said in a small voice. "I suppose that makes sense. I still don't trust him, though. He's thwarted all of my plans."

"Well," Ming asked, "what are you going to do now?"

Francis perked up a little. "I've found a new recruit," he said.

The next evening, once the zoo was closed, Francis prepared to set his new plan into action. Ming's nerves tingled inside her as she worked up the courage to say something that she'd been wanting to ask Francis all day. Now, as he squeezed through the bars, she had run out of time. It was now or never.

"I want to come with you!" she blurted.

"What?" Francis spluttered.

"What?" Tang echoed. "Not again, Ming. It's not safe for you."

"I want to come with you to the aviary," she said. She took a breath and looked Francis in the eye. "I'd like to be free again," she said. "Just one last time."

"I would love your help, Ming, but the door is locked. How will you break out?"

"She could always bang her head against it again," Tang suggested dryly. "As that worked so well last time."

Ming shot a look at Tang as he chuckled to himself.

"Maybe there is a way," Francis mumbled. "I'll be back."

He disappeared in the direction of Monkey Hill, and Ming felt her stomach drop. "He's not going to come back this time, is he?" she said quietly.

"Why do you always think everyone is going to leave you?" Tang asked. "I never have."

Ming snorted. "That's because you have no choice. You're stuck with me."

"Who left you?" Tang asked.

"My family," Ming replied. She felt a sob build in her throat and wiped at her eyes, turning so that Tang wouldn't make fun of her again.

After a pause, he said, "They didn't leave you, Ming. You were taken from them. It was the same for me and all the other animals here. Most of them were taken from their homes. But we can build new homes, new families. Like you and me…and even Francis. We can be each other's family."

Ming didn't know what to say. She had never heard Tang talk like this before. Never thought that he might feel exactly the same way she did. She had been so lonely that she had ignored him, and it turned out that he was just as lonely as she was.

"I'm back!" Francis puffed.

There was a giggle from the other side of the door and scratching at the metal. Then there was the distinctive sliding noise as the bolt was released and pulled across. Ming placed a paw on the handle. It slid open easily. There in front of her sat Chiney and Jacky, looking very pleased with themselves.

"I asked them to escape again," Francis explained. "One last time."

Ming paused at the door. "Tang, come with us."

"No, I think I'll stay here and catch up on my sleep," he said. "But I'll be here when you get back."

Ming looked at Tang for a moment, her breath caught in her throat, then she gave him a small smile. "Thank you, Tang," she replied.

CHAPTER 12

FRANCIS

September 20, 1940

There was something in the air, Francis thought, as he, Ming, and the monkeys headed for the giant aviary. It was like the moment before a storm broke, when you could feel it building, the atmosphere buzzing. He hoped it meant that soon, everything would be all right. He would have done all he could to ensure that the message was delivered and his beloved country was safe.

Francis had spent some time talking with Toca earlier that day, keeping to the shady spots so that he wouldn't be spotted by any humans. He had gone over the route with Toca again and again until she knew it as well as her own beak. He had warned her about the pillboxes and told her to stay away from the humans as much as possible, instructing her to fly over less-populated areas. Aside from her size, the one thing that differentiated Toca from Francis was her coloring. Nobody noticed a dull gray pigeon flying in their midst, but a toucan would be a little harder to ignore.

"Are you all right?" Ming whispered as they neared the aviary.

"I need this to work," Francis said. "The attack on London could be imminent. This may be our last chance, and I'm not sure I can entirely trust Toca, but what other choice do I have?"

Ming glanced up at the sky nervously. "Francis, what will happen if the enemy succeeds? What will become of us here in the zoo?"

Francis paused, forcing the words out. "If they blitz London?"

Ming nodded, her eyes reflecting the fear that he felt twisting deep in his gut.

Francis couldn't think of an answer that could put Ming's mind at ease...or his own. If he told her the truth, that the Nazis had the power to destroy everything and everyone in their path, he knew she would never sleep again.

He forced a smile and said, "It won't come to that."

They reached the aviary. It was a large brick enclosure with a huge net draped from towering posts that hung over it like a circus tent. It was filled with an array of exotic birds, some bigger than Toca—cranes with magnificent spiked yellow crests upon their heads, and hornbills—then smaller birds like kookaburras and bright blue-and-yellow sunbirds. Most of them were perched atop branches and ledges within the aviary, their heads nestled beneath their wings as they settled down to roost for the night. Toca, though, stood guard at the aviary's entrance at the side.

She had her back to them as they approached and spun round, startled when Chiney giggled nervously.

"It's only us," Francis reassured her, feeling as on edge as Toca looked.

Toca waited for Chiney to pick the lock. Unlike Ming and Tang's enclosure, this one had a heavy wooden door with a simple bolt, secured with a metal padlock.

"Chiney's becoming a pro at this," Ming observed as the lock clicked open within a few breaths.

"Why is *the panda* here?" Toca asked, eyeing Ming suspiciously.

"I—I'm here to help," Ming stuttered.

Toca waited patiently for a while, then turned to Francis as the door remained closed. "Now what?"

"Don't look at us," Jacky replied. "We only said we could *unlock* the door. We're not strong enough to actually *open* it."

Francis felt as though he had been shot out of the sky all over again. How could he have been so stupid? Of *course* none of them would be able to open the door. The monkeys, skilled as they were, were slight things. Even an entire troupe of them couldn't haul the heavy oak door open to let Toca out, and Francis couldn't exactly pull it open with his beak.

"Ahem," Ming cleared her throat beside him.

"Not now, Ming, I'm trying to think."

"AHEM!" Ming coughed again.

"Ming, I really can't—" Francis slapped a wing to his head. "Ming, *you* could open the door!"

"That's what I've been trying to tell you," she said, rolling her eyes exactly as Tang would have done.

"I told you I was here to help," she said to Toca.

She didn't wait for an apology. She gripped the handle with her paws, opening the door as quickly and quietly as she could.

The aviary was older than many of the other enclosures and in disrepair. The hinges on the door had rusted and crumbled away in some places. Francis winced as it screeched and screamed its way open as if in protest.

The sound awoke some of the birds, who screeched and fluttered their wings.

"It's all right!" Francis whispered, trying to hush the noise. "We're not here to hurt you."

A pair of small lovebirds flew to the ground and looked up at Francis, both cocking their heads, their eyes narrowed suspiciously. "What are you here for? You want to join us?"

Francis shuddered at the thought of being trapped forever. "No, we are just..."

Toca stepped toward the birds and they hopped back as she loomed over them. "It is none of your business," she growled in a low voice.

The lovebirds shook their feathers at her indignantly, but they flew back to their perch. After that, the other birds quieted. Francis noticed that none of them seemed to care that Toca was making an escape.

Toca checked that the coast was clear, then stepped out, not looking back.

"Do you want to say goodbye?" Francis asked.

Toca trilled a quiet laugh. "Why would I want to do that?" she asked. "I'll be glad to see the back of this prison."

"But your friends," Ming added. "Won't you miss them?"

The birds in the aviary suddenly grew very quiet. None of them seemed to want to say goodbye to Toca, either.

"What is there to miss?" Toca snapped. She strode away from the aviary into an open clearing.

Ming exchanged a look with Chiney and Jacky behind Toca's back, but Francis ignored them. They had come this far. They couldn't change their plans now because Toca was a little unpopular.

"Ready?" Francis asked, noticing that Toca's feathers were trembling slightly.

She nodded. "I can do this," she said, flapping her wings a few times as though testing them out. "It's been a while since I've flown any distance other than back and forth in the aviary, but I could never forget how to fly."

She jumped slightly as though about to take off. "Wait!" Francis called. "Don't forget the message."

Toca looked slightly annoyed. "Of course," she said. "Silly me."

She swiped the red capsule out of Francis's wing, clutching it tightly within her sharp, curved claws. Then, without another word, she took to the sky so suddenly that she almost knocked Francis over.

"Something's not right with that bird," Ming warned. "Did you see the way the other birds looked at her? Are you sure you can trust her?"

Francis suddenly realized that he really wasn't sure. He had been so desperate that someone could deliver the message that he hadn't been as cautious as he should have been. He watched anxiously as Toca gained height. Suddenly the air-raid sirens wailed, catching Toca off guard. She faltered for a moment, almost losing her grip on the capsule, but quickly recovered.

"It's not safe out here in the open," Ming said.

But Francis remained where he was, watching Toca fly farther and farther away, in the wrong direction. Toward Germany.

"No!" he shouted. "Toca, that's the wrong way!"

Ming, Jacky, and Chiney stood beside Francis, the four of them watching as Toca ducked and dove through the sky. She soared low for a moment, flying right above them, then called out a single word, "Sorry," before heading off.

A furious fire ignited within Francis as any chance of delivering his message slipped further from his grasp.

"I have to stop her!" he cried. He ripped off his bandage with his beak, then took off, chasing after Toca as fast as his injured wing would allow, fear and adrenaline pushing him on.

"Francis!" Ming shouted, but she was far, far below, Jacky and Chiney beside her just small blurs bouncing up and down.

Francis flew on, surprised at how well his wing was holding up. His shoulder felt stiff and sore, but it was more of a dull ache. He was flying again! The joy of it was overtaken by a regret that he hadn't tried one last time to deliver the message himself before trusting Toca.

Below, the humans ran for cover. In London, the closest and safest places to hide were the underground train stations, but some humans used their basements if they had one, like the staff at the zoo. Others had temporary shelters made from curved steel panels dug into the ground at the end of their gardens. From this high up, Francis thought that they looked like silvery wood lice stuck in the mud.

He scanned the sky for Toca. He was gaining on her now, and she didn't seem to know that he was in pursuit. He used the same tactic that the air force sometimes used and flew higher, planning to attack from above so that she wouldn't see him coming. But as he rose, an almighty sound roared directly ahead.

Messerschmitts.

Toca faltered, startled by the appearance of so many fighter planes. Francis refocused his energy. He had the upper hand now, being used to flying through such extreme conditions. He wouldn't be so easily deterred.

Below, the bombing began. Huge missiles fell from the sky in quick succession, whistling as they dropped lower, lower, lower, then hit their target with an enormous blast that threw both Francis and Toca off course.

The sky filled with black smoke from the explosions below and the planes above. Francis glanced back. The zoo was far away now, Regent's Park barely in sight. The enemy planes kept coming, and then suddenly, as if out of nowhere, there were Spitfires. The Royal Air Force, preparing to wage battle in the sky.

And Francis and Toca were caught up in the very eye of the storm.

As furious as he was at Toca for betraying him, Francis could see that the toucan was struggling. She flew in ever-decreasing circles, disoriented by the noise and the smoke and the planes. He had to lead her back to the zoo. Maybe he could force her to land and make her realize she was wrong.

He flew on, pushing his injured wing to its limit, even though the searing pain had returned and his whole wing burned. Toca was flying much lower to the ground now, trying to get away from the chaos all around her. But that meant that she was in danger of being hit by the groundsmen below, a blast from the bombs, or flying into one of the barrage balloon's wires. She knew nothing about the dangers of war, dangers that were hidden in plain view all around them, like a tiger waiting to strike its prey.

Francis closed in until he was only feet away from Toca.

"Toca!" he yelled, hoping she could hear him over the rattle of gunfire and the thunderous cracks of the bombs landing.

She glanced backward, startled for a moment, but then flapped faster.

"Toca!" Francis shouted again, trying to compete with her much larger wingspan. "Just drop the capsule," he begged. "If all you wanted was to escape, you've done that. The capsule means nothing to you."

She ignored him, but she seemed to be tiring. Some birds were not made for long distances, Francis knew; maybe toucans were one of them. She soared for a moment on the wind, heading back in the direction of Regent's Park and giving Francis the opportunity to catch up. He swooped down in front of her, cutting her off so that she had to frantically flap again to stop herself from dropping out of the sky.

Toca looked terrified and exhausted as she searched for an escape. But Francis and Toca both knew by now that although he was the smaller bird, he could outlast her in the sky.

"I just wanted to be free," she cried. "Is that so terrible?"

Francis shook his head. "Of course not. But why did you take the capsule? You could have left without it."

"I knew you would only let me out of the aviary if I

promised to help you. I had to take the capsule in case you changed your mind and locked me back up."

Francis felt ashamed of himself. She was probably right. He was so focused on his mission that he didn't stop to consider the other animals in the zoo. He'd only thought of those who would be helpful to him.

"I just want the capsule back," Francis said. "Please, Toca. You know how important it is."

"No!" Toca screamed. "I can't. If I land now, I'll be caught. I don't want to go back there, Francis."

"Pass me the capsule, then," Francis asked, reaching out a claw.

Toca's talons tightened around the capsule, and Francis could see the terror in her eyes. "I can't," she said. "I don't want to fall."

Francis's mind raced. His hurt wing was tiring. He had to get the capsule back. His only option seemed to be to wait for Toca's wings to fail her, but despite everything, he didn't want to do that. There was only one more option. He'd have to grab it. He darted at her without thinking, his eyes trained only on the capsule held within her grasp. Toca screamed and swerved to one side. Francis attacked again, this time managing to catch

hold of the end of the capsule within his beak, but Toca pulled away, yanking it away from him. "Stop! You'll kill us both!"

The zoo was directly below now. Francis could make out Ming and the monkeys watching as he and Toca waged a battle of their own, below the planes. His wing began to seize up, so that Francis flew slightly lopsided. Time was running out. He didn't have long until it gave out altogether. He opened his beak wide and, with a loud war cry, dove at Toca, knocking them both into a spin. Their wings and claws became entangled as they both struggled to break free, sending a flurry of feathers through the air as the solid, unforgiving ground rose up faster and faster to greet them.

At the last moment, they separated. Toca managed to swoop up and out of the tailspin, soaring back into the sky, heading for the trees. But for Francis it was too late. He could only close his eyes as he waited for impact.

CHAPTER 13
MING

September 20, 1940

Ming watched in horror as Francis plunged from the sky. In the distance, the cacophony of sirens and bombs continued, but the noise was drowned out by the sound of her heartbeat pulsing inside her ears.

"We have to do something!" she cried desperately.

Some of the other monkeys had come to watch the two birds fighting in the sky. Chiney and Jacky pulled them into a tight huddle.

"What are you doing?" Ming asked as one by one the monkeys climbed on top of each other, forming what looked like the base of a pyramid.

"No time to explain!" Jacky shouted as he clambered up the tower of monkeys.

Francis hurtled through the air, getting closer and closer. The monkeys all looked up, adjusting their position this way and that while Jacky shouted out commands. Those on the very top linked their arms and tails together into a makeshift net. There was a sudden whoosh and the monkey tower wavered slightly as Francis landed within their grasp. Miraculously, the tower held firm.

Ming hurried over as the monkeys carefully dismounted, leaving Chiney and Jacky holding Francis in the middle of the circle.

"Is he...?" Ming began.

Chiney lowered his head as Jacky gently lay Francis on the ground.

"Francis?" Jacky whispered. "Can you hear me?"

Francis's wing twitched. He opened his eyes with a groan, then tried to sit up, his feathers trembling.

"You have got to stop falling out of the sky," Ming tried to joke. "Are you all right?" She checked him over for any signs of blood or broken bones.

He held his healing wing awkwardly, but apart from that appeared to be in one piece.

Chiney pointed to the treetops marking the boundary of the zoo. "The toucan went that way," he said. "The traitor!"

"We'll go after her," Jacky said as a few of the monkeys nodded. "We'll find her and get the capsule back for you."

Francis shook his head frantically. Jacky and Chiney stared as Francis lowered his head in his wings.

"I'm so sorry, Francis," Ming whispered, her voice breaking. "Please...say something."

She knew how hard he had tried—putting his life at risk so that he could deliver that message. But now it was gone and had taken all of Ming's hope with it. As some of the monkeys returned to Monkey Hill with their tails trailing between their legs, she knew she wasn't the only one who felt that way.

Francis coughed and spluttered as though he were about to be sick, and Ming stepped back. She watched as he bobbed his head back and forth, making a half-choking, half-gasping sound.

Ming lifted a paw to pat Francis on the back as he opened his beak wide. Something red appeared. He continued coughing and the thing emerged from his throat in one piece.

"The capsule!" Jacky cried. "He has it!"

"You have it?" Ming laughed. "You have the capsule! I thought you were choking to death."

Francis smiled grimly. "A little trick I picked up from an owl I met during training."

"What do we do now?" Ming asked.

Francis looked up at her. "We?"

She nodded and so did Jacky and Chiney. "Yes, we. We want to help. What can we do?"

Francis lifted his reinjured wing. "I'm not sure there is much I can do until this is healed," he said. "We seem to be out of options."

"That treacherous toucan!" Chiney snarled. "Was she a spy, Francis?"

"I have half a mind to go after her," Jacky agreed.

"She wasn't a spy," Francis replied. "She just wanted to be free and made some wrong choices." He smiled at Chiney and Jacky. "You two have done more than enough to help me, but the risk is too high. The mission was given to me, and I must be the one to complete it. Alone."

The monkeys glanced at each other, remaining silent.

He was right, Ming thought. The humans were already keeping a closer eye on the monkeys after their numerous escape acts. She would offer to take the message herself if she thought there was any way a giant panda could travel through London undetected. Francis looked worse than he had when he'd first landed in her enclosure almost two weeks ago, utterly broken.

"Get some rest," she suggested. "I think you should let Jean look at your wing in the morning, then we can think of a new plan."

She expected Francis to argue or come up with another feather-brained scheme, but he walked slowly toward the giant panda enclosure, his bad wing dragging along the ground beside him.

"He needs a little time," Ming told the monkeys who watched him leave.

"We're still here for him if he needs help," Jacky said.

"I know," Ming replied. "Thank you for saving him."

Ming bid them farewell, then followed after Francis. Despite what he'd said about doing it alone, he still needed her help. There had to be another way to deliver the message. If Francis was out of ideas, then she'd have to come up with one herself.

Francis slept through the night, despite the bombing, which only stopped when the sun rose. He snuggled up with the capsule beneath his good wing and barely stirred even as explosions echoed around the zoo like a thunderstorm. He was exhausted, Ming thought, wishing she were able to sleep so easily. The incident with Toca had upset her more than she'd realized. At the time she'd barely had a moment to breathe, let alone take in what was happening, but now the incident replayed over and over in her head. The way Toca and Francis had fought. The way Francis had fallen out of the sky, as limp as a rag. Ming's heart raced again just thinking of what might have happened if it hadn't had been for the monkeys' quick thinking.

There was a familiar click and clang as Jean hurried in, her face red and flustered as she shouted at someone on the other side of the door. She saw Ming watching and stood in front of her protectively.

"I won't let you do this!" Jean cried. "Not again. They are not museum exhibits! They have already traveled to and from Whipsnade once. It's not an easy journey. You could make them very ill...or worse!"

Ming's blood froze as the voice came in reply. "It is not up to you," the boss said. "I have made the executive decision to evacuate the giant pandas. They are two of our most valuable assets. It's no longer safe for them here in London."

"They are living creatures, not assets!" Jean yelled.

In the corner of the enclosure, Tang and Francis awoke to see what all the fuss was about.

"Tang!" Ming hissed. "They want to take us away again."

"Away?" Tang mumbled, rubbing his eyes. "Away where?"

Ming looked at Francis, realizing that he was in clear view. "Francis, hide!"

Francis ducked beneath the straw, but his tiny black eyes peered out.

Jean backed away, looking defeated as two men holding large sticks entered the enclosure. They tried to usher Tang toward the open doorway, but he refused to move.

"Stay firm," he told Ming. "We'll not be so easily moved this time. London Zoo is our home. I want to stay here...with you."

"So do I," Ming realized, and sat on the floor with a determined thud. However she had come to be there, the zoo was her home, with people she cared about—Jean, the monkeys, Francis, Tang. Maybe if they just ignored the men, they might go away? It wasn't as though they could really force them to move. It would take more than two humans to drag two giant pandas out of their enclosure.

They seemed to be at an impasse. The boss pulled one of the men aside and whispered to him as time seemed to slow. Ming watched as the man reached beneath his shirt and pulled out a tranquilizer gun loaded with a dart. The last time Ming had seen one of those was when she was a tiny cub living in China. She screamed, stricken with fear. Francis reared up from his pile of straw, launching himself at the man and pecking at his ankles. Jean rushed forward to help, but the boss held her back.

"Run!" Francis yelled over the commotion.

Ming looked at Tang and they both seemed to come to the same conclusion. There was no escape. And if the boss got his hands on Francis...on the message, then...

The man knocked Francis to the ground. Ming tried to help, but the man moved swiftly. He pointed the gun at Tang and then at Ming, and with two swift shots, hit them both. They dropped to the ground in quick succession.

Jean sobbed quietly as Ming's vision blurred in and out of focus. Tang lay still beside her, his tongue lolling out of the side of his mouth. As the world began to spin and fade into darkness, the last thing Ming saw was Francis mouthing a single promise: "I will find you."

CHAPTER 14
FRANCIS

September 24, 1940

Francis had taken refuge in Monkey Hill. Ming and Tang were gone. Perhaps for good. It was like losing George all over again, except this time Francis was the one left behind. In the end, the emptiness became too much to bear, so he joined Chiney and Jacky. He was torn between his promise to find Ming and Tang and completing his mission. He could perhaps make the long journey mostly on foot to Bletchley. But the thought of Ming and Tang stopped him from leaving, like an anchor pulling at his gut every time he drew closer to the edge of the zoo.

The monkeys had tried to cheer him up with their tumbles and acrobatics, but when they could barely bring more than a sigh from Francis, they left him alone. He settled himself at the very bottom of Monkey Hill, nestled within the smallest of crags. He felt safe there, secure. He gazed at the sky at night, wondering what he should do next. He desperately needed to deliver his message, but since Ming and Tang had been taken away, he had lost some of his fight...his determination. He wouldn't even be alive now if it weren't for Ming and Jean.

He finally came to a decision. He needed to know that Ming and Tang were safe before he continued on his mission. For that, he would need to devise a new plan: how to get to Whipsnade Zoo.

"There you are!" a voice hissed, startling Francis from his nap.

Francis tried to escape, but he had become so tightly wedged into his hiding place that he could only shuffle forward an inch before soft, warm hands enveloped him, gently pulling him out of his nest.

Jean examined Francis closely. "I've been so worried about you," she said. "I thought that my father might have scared you off for good. Let me look at that wing."

She carried Francis out of the monkeys' enclosure. Francis smiled at Jacky and Chiney to reassure them he would be fine. Jean slipped Francis beneath her jacket, sending him into a dull darkness.

"Sorry," she said. "I don't want anyone to see you."

A few minutes later, Jean opened her jacket, blinding Francis with bright sunlight, which shone through the small window. They were in the back room of the giant panda enclosure again, where Jean had first treated him.

She carefully placed him on the desk and inspected his bad wing, gently lifting it up and down, left and right. The pain had faded to a dull ache, and although Francis felt as though he could probably fly again, he was nervous. His last two experiences hadn't turned out so well.

Jean sighed and knelt down to look Francis in the eye. "I miss Ming and Tang, too," she said. "That's why you're still here, isn't it?"

Francis cooed quietly in response and Jean nodded. She filled a bowl with warm water and cleaned his feathers. This time the water turned a murky brown and Francis felt slightly embarrassed that he couldn't remember the last time he'd had a bath.

When Jean finished, she pulled out a chair and sat down, handing Francis a handful of seed. She produced her own lunch from a tin container, breaking off a piece of her sandwich for Francis before she ate the rest. The two ate in a companionable silence and, not for the first time, Francis wished that he had a way to communicate with the humans so that he could be sure that Ming was safe and tell Jean about the message. Sometimes he had made gestures to George and it felt as though he had actually understood what Francis meant. Maybe he could do the same with Jean? Despite the fact that she was the boss's daughter, he knew that she was a good human, and Francis was sure he could trust her.

He glanced up at the wall at a black-and-white photograph of a small panda cub that he presumed was Ming. Beside it was a map of the zoo. He studied it, but something wasn't quite right. Some things were out of place, or not there at all, like the lion enclosure and the penguin pool. He stepped closer for a better look, then saw that a square area had been circled with a red pen, right beside the elephant house. Francis jumped up and tapped his beak on the circle, trying to get Jean's attention.

"What is it?" Jean asked, putting her sandwich down.

Francis jumped again, tapping the photograph of Ming, then hopped to the side to jump up and tap the map. She watched Francis jump up and down a few more times with a puzzled expression on her face, and just when Francis was about to give up, she smiled.

"Ming!" she said. "Is that what you want to know?"

Francis almost collapsed with relief. He bobbed his head up and down as Jean stared at him, awestruck. "You really are a remarkable pigeon."

She pointed to the map. "This is our sister zoo, Whipsnade."

She opened a drawer, pulling out a larger map, and swiped her lunch to one side so that she could open it out fully on the desk. "This is where we are," she said, pointing at London. "This is where Whipsnade is. Where Ming and Tang are."

Francis hopped onto the spot on the map where Regent's Park was. Bletchley Park was slightly off to the north, Francis estimated about fifty miles away. If his wing was good and his path clear, he could probably make the journey in just over an hour. He bent to see where Whipsnade was in comparison.

For the first time since Ming had been taken away, Francis smiled. The other zoo was only a fifteen-minute journey from Bletchley, if even that.

Francis tested his wing, seeing if he could raise it. It was a little stiff, but less painful than he had been expecting. Jean realized what he was trying to do. "Just go slowly," she cautioned him. "The break seems to be healed, but your muscles have grown weaker from lack of exercise."

Francis lifted his head to the window.

"How about we try it out?" Jean asked.

She carried Francis outside, behind the enclosure where there would be no prying eyes, then set Francis down on the ground.

"Ready?" she asked.

Francis clenched his beak and slowly flapped. He had done it before, he could do it again, he thought. His heart raced as he thought of how helpless he had felt when his wing had failed him. He shook his head determinedly. That wouldn't happen this time. As long as he took his time and went slowly...

Without even thinking, he found himself in the air. He took Jean's advice, trying not to push his wings too much, but he had forgotten the feeling of flying for the joy of it, and he was soon ducking and diving, circling overhead as Jean whooped and laughed below. Francis quickly retrieved the capsule from where he'd hidden it inside Ming's enclosure, then set off. He landed in an oak tree, surveying the zoo for one last time, and then flew north, toward Bletchley.

CHAPTER 15
MING

September 21, 1940

There was a loud pounding. Ming tried to work out where it was coming from as she opened her eyes blearily. Then she realized that she was no longer at home, and that the pounding that reverberated in her ears and set her teeth on edge was coming from her own head.

"Francis?" she called out groggily. "Tang?"

She lifted her head, and the ground spun beneath her. She lay back down, staring at the floor. Wherever she was, it was quiet...well, a lot quieter than she was used to. There were no sounds of nearby city traffic or the humans making their way excitedly from one enclosure to another. There were no sounds of Tang snoring beside her. And there was no Francis.

Ming had always believed that she hated the noise of the zoo. How it never seemed to cease, day or night. But now that all she could hear was the gentle rustling of leaves blowing in the breeze and the occasional twitter of birdcall, Ming found she hated the quiet more.

She forced herself up and took in her surroundings. She was in a smaller enclosure than she was used to. This one had no thick metal bars or walls. It was simple, hastily put together with wooden posts rammed into the earth and wire mesh acting as a fence. A large building loomed to the left, and Ming realized that she knew where she was. A loud trumpeting sound from the elephant house a moment later confirmed her suspicions.

She was back at Whipsnade Zoo.

Water and bamboo had been left for her inside the cage, and despite feeling utterly sick with her pounding head, she forced herself to eat and drink. She had no idea how long she'd been out, and no idea if she was to stay at Whipsnade or if they would be moving her somewhere else. She chomped down on the bamboo, chewing it for as long as she could, then forced herself to swallow it, even though her stomach gurgled in protest. Suddenly, she noticed a large black-and-white lump lurking beneath a blanket in the corner.

"Tang?"

Ming moved closer, afraid at how still and quiet the figure was. Tang usually made more noise when he slept than he did awake. She moved closer still, watching his back for any movement, any signs of life. She held out a trembling paw, intending to gently pat him, when the lump moved all of a sudden. Two black-ringed eyes stood facing her, familiar, but not. It was a giant panda all right, but not Tang.

"Who are you?" the giant panda demanded.

"I—I'm Ming," she stuttered. "Who are you? Where have they taken Tang?"

The other giant panda narrowed her eyes. "What is Tang?" she asked. "And what are you doing in my enclosure?"

"I'm from London Zoo," Ming replied, backing away slightly as the giant panda continued to glare in a not so friendly way. "They knocked us out—Tang and I—then I woke up here. Were you evacuated, too?" Ming couldn't remember there being another giant panda at Whipsnade when she'd last been there, but then, she hadn't been there very long and had been kept in a brick building, so she hadn't been able to see very much at all.

The other giant panda's eyes softened slightly. "I'm

Sung. I heard about you the last time you were here—there was such excitement that the famous Ming was coming to stay. I've always lived here, but I think they wanted to keep us apart in case there was any kind of rivalry between us."

"Rivalry?" Ming asked. "Over what?"

Sung gestured her head to the back of the enclosure. It went off slightly to the right, out of sight behind a low wall. Sung nodded at Ming to go ahead, and Ming turned the corner where there were three separate sleeping areas constructed from wooden crates. The first two were empty, but in the last was a snuffling, snoring lump.

"Tang!" Ming cried, amazed that she hadn't heard him sooner.

She suddenly realized what Sung had meant. "The humans thought that you and I might fight over *Tang*?"

Ming didn't know if she was still feeling the effects from the tranquilizer, but she burst into hysterical laughter, waking him.

"What are you so happy about?" Tang asked, looking from Ming to Sung. He rubbed his paws over his eyes. "Am I seeing double?"

Ming glanced at Sung, who rolled her eyes, and burst into laughter all over again.

They were interrupted by the sound of marching feet.

Ming and Sung looked out through the wire fence to see a group of humans—men and boys—parading up and down. Many of the men were holding strange objects like broom handles, spades, and garden hoes, while the boys held sticks, resting over their shoulders.

"What are they doing?" Ming asked. She'd seen humans do some strange things in her time, but never something this unusual. "Have they gone mad?"

Sung snorted. "They call themselves the Home Guard," she explained. "The male humans who were too old or too young to be sent into service formed their own little army unit, to keep us and the other humans safe while the soldiers fight on the front lines."

Ming was unconvinced. "How can a bunch of old men with garden implements keep us safe?"

The parade was followed by a large group of children, who skipped along behind singing a song. It suddenly struck Ming that she hadn't seen so many children in such a long time.

Sung saw her watching the children and said, "They were evacuated here from London, too. Many of them are the children of your zookeepers."

"Does that mean we are safe here?" Ming asked.

Sung sat down with a sigh. "Supposedly. Although we haven't been entirely missed by the Nazis."

She indicated a shallow pond in a grassy paddock opposite their enclosure. A couple of ducks swam leisurely across it, while two giraffes—one adult, one no more than a few months old—chewed the leaves from a nearby tree. "That pond wasn't always there," Sung continued. "A bomb landed one night and that's the crater it left behind. It slowly filled up with rainwater. There are others, too. The humans are keeping them as ponds. It's too much hard work to keep filling them in."

Ming felt uneasy. She'd been dragged away from her home and sent to Whipsnade to keep her safe. But how safe were any of them when the Nazis were planning such a big attack?

The Home Guard returned, then set to work in a field beside the giraffe house. Ming noticed that there were fewer animal enclosures than when she'd last been there, and many of the paddocks had been turned into vegetable patches. There were even chickens and a couple of goats wandering around. Ming felt like she was in more of a farm than a zoo.

"They work hard, the humans," Sung said. "If it

wasn't for them growing all the food here, we would be a lot hungrier. They've grown enough to keep animals' and humans' bellies full."

"What's that?" Ming asked, pointing to a building at the top of the hill.

"That's the fellows' pavilion. They've turned it into an air-raid defense post. You can see across the countryside for miles from up there," Sung said. "Or so I've heard." She gestured to the wire mesh.

"Maybe one day we can take a look for ourselves?" Ming suggested, only half joking.

"I think you've done enough wandering, don't you?" Tang asked.

Sung looked at Tang, then back to Ming expectantly.

Ming sighed. "Our keeper, Jean, forgot to lock our enclosure one evening, so a friend and I took a stroll around the zoo. Tang was too much of a coward to join us."

"I was not!" Tang cried indignantly. "I was being the sensible one. Someone has to be, with you and Francis and the monkeys causing all kinds of commotion."

"Francis?" Sung asked. "Is he another panda?"

Ming shook her head. "He's a very important

pigeon. He works for the National Pigeon Service and was taking a message to the humans to be decoded. But he didn't make it."

Sung gasped. "Oh no! I'm so sorry."

Tang laughed. "He didn't die! He was shot out of the sky by a spy plane and landed in our enclosure. He's spent the last few weeks trying to find someone else to deliver the blasted message for him. It's caused nothing but trouble."

Sung sat quietly for a while, seeming lost in thought. She glanced up at Ming. "What was the message about?"

"Ming," Tang warned. "It's supposed to be a secret."

"I won't tell anyone," Sung huffed. "Besides, who *could* I tell? It's only us here."

Ming wondered if she should tell the truth. Since she'd found out what the Nazis were planning, she hadn't been able to think of anything else. But wasn't it better that Sung could be prepared for the worst?

"The Nazis are planning to blitz London," Ming blurted out. "The air raids have been bad, but nothing compared to what the Nazis will do in a full-out attack."

Sung's eyes went wide.

"It won't come to that," Tang tried to reassure her.

"Francis will deliver the message and our troops will be ready."

He looked to Ming and she nodded, even though she had no idea what Francis's plan was now. The fate of London, perhaps Great Britain, weighed on his shoulders. She wished she were still with him to help in some way.

The sky had begun to darken, and Ming was surprised at how quickly the day had gone by. In London Zoo the days often dragged, but here with two giant pandas for company, the time flew. Sung and Ming headed for their beds, with Sung taking the one at the opposite end to Tang's and Ming taking the one in the middle. Tang was already snoring, but for once the noise didn't bother Ming. It felt comforting having two friends beside her. She wondered if Francis would ever manage to deliver his message and if she'd ever see him again.

Her eyelids slowly drooped, and she soon found herself falling asleep, when she was rudely awoken by sirens. They sounded different than the ones in London; these were slightly echoey and distorted.

"What is that?" she asked Sung, who had awoken beside her.

"Wolves," Sung told her. "They howl whenever the

sirens go off. Sometimes they howl before the sirens start. Almost as though they can sense danger approaching."

Ming listened. The wolves' howls sounded full of sorrow, as though they were calling out for lost loved ones who never returned. *I know how they feel*, Ming thought sadly.

CHAPTER 16
FRANCIS

September 25, 1940

It had been almost six months since Francis had last seen his home at Bletchley, but as he flew, he barely had to think about which direction he was flying in. It was the natural homing instinct that every pigeon has—no matter where they were, even if they were lost, injured, or confused, they would always find their way home. He wondered if George had also somehow found his way home, but he knew that the chances of that were unlikely.

Francis soared lower, preparing for landing. Bletchley was a huge, sprawling mansion on luscious grounds. Along with the mansion, there were a number of huts, each housing intelligence officers and code breakers, who worked on messages and codes from various different sources. Francis had sneaked into one once and had seen curious machines that looked like typewriters. When the humans pressed one of the keys, a small lamp lit up. He'd later learned that they were called Enigma machines and were used to decipher coded German messages.

He continued on, over the trees and the long winding road that led to his home, then there it was! Bletchley. Standing proudly in the middle of the countryside. Francis was suddenly overcome with emotion. To him, Bletchley meant so many things—not only home, but family, friends, and a sense of pride that came with working alongside the humans and, in some small way, making a difference. What Francis and the other pigeons did here was important. Their actions could alter the course of history, could even bring an end to the war.

Francis took a deep breath, pushing down the sob that had built deep down in his chest and was trying to force its way out.

He had made it!

After all this time, not knowing whether he would

even survive. After all of his thwarted efforts to deliver the message and complete his mission. He had done it! Whatever happened now, he couldn't help but feel a sense of pride—and then fear that he might be too late. That everything he had gone through had been for nothing.

He flew to the east, where his loft came into view. The entrance was a small open window in a redbrick building above the stables. Francis swooped inside, landing with an immense feeling of relief.

His foot caught a wire running across the coop, tripping an alarm somewhere in the building. There was the faint tinkle of a ringing bell, and Francis set the red capsule down in front of him and waited. A few moments later, there was a rapid thud of footsteps on the wooden steps, and a soldier from the Signal Corps appeared, slightly flushed.

"Francis!" he said, recognizing the pigeon. "We thought you were lost!"

He stroked Francis's head and dipped a hand into his jacket pocket, pulling out a handful of seeds and scattering them. Then he picked up the battered red capsule and examined it, his brow furrowed.

"How did you remove this from your leg?" he muttered,

examining the fastener, which was mangled and twisted from where Ming had hastily chewed on it.

The man scratched his head, then put the red capsule in his pocket. "I'll take this to the code breakers. Well done, Francis!"

The man disappeared back the way he came, and Francis released a long sigh. His journey was over. His mission complete. There was only one more thing he had to do: fly to Whipsnade and find Ming. He walked over to the window, looking out over the grounds, then back at the loft, but something felt different. Like it wasn't home any longer. Something pulled at his gut, and his wings shook as though urging Francis in another direction.

Still, he needed to know that he had accomplished something. That his efforts had not all been in vain.

That he wasn't too late.

He hopped down the wooden steps into the stable, where he passed beneath a couple of horses, avoiding their hooves and backsides. Then he went through a door, leading to the offices where some of the top intelligence officers worked. He flew through a window to where the huts stood in neat rows. Francis caught sight of the soldier who had taken his message entering one of the huts at the far end. He waited, hiding around the side of the building until the man reemerged. Then Francis hurried over, jumping onto the windowsill where the window was slightly ajar, and poked his head in.

One of the code breakers had already opened the capsule and unrolled the message. There were four columns, each with a row of five letters or numbers. At the top of the paper the words *Pigeon Service* were written, and the bottom of the paper was signed with the messy scrawl of the lieutenant general's signature. The code breaker reached over to a pile of books, carefully selected one, and then opened it, comparing the code on the message to the code in the book. Francis thought that the code breaker must be one of the very best, because it didn't take her long to decipher the message. She wrote it down on another piece of paper, then turned to her colleague.

"Prime Minister Churchill needs to see this at once," she said, voice urgent.

Francis frowned. When he'd left Bletchley to go to France, Neville Chamberlain had been prime minister. He brushed the confusion away and listened to what the woman was saying. "There's to be an attack on London," she said. "Imminently. They plan to target Saint Paul's Cathedral and everything surrounding it. They plan to blitz London."

A deathly hush fell over the room. After a few breaths, the woman snatched up the message and ran off toward the mansion. Francis briefly wondered if the new prime minister was there, when the image of the map he'd stolen with Chiney and Jacky came to mind. Saint Paul's Cathedral was only a few miles from Regent's Park. If the Nazis intended to make that area their primary target, the zoo was sure to be hit.

Francis's mind raced. If he had been one day later, his message might have been too late. But the threat was still very real. He had promised Ming he would find her, but she was safe (or as safe as anyone could be in the middle of the war) at Whipsnade. But when the Nazis blitzed London...Francis couldn't bear to think of the consequences. Jean and the other humans might stand a chance—they had their shelters, after all—but the animals were trapped. There was nothing they would be able to do to keep safe, nowhere they could go to wait out the battle.

They were sitting targets.

As much as it pained Francis to leave Ming behind when she was so close by, he had a duty to those other animals who he had come to consider friends. Jacky and Chiney and the other monkeys had saved him more than once. He couldn't abandon them now when they needed his help.

He eased his head from the gap in the window but suddenly found himself being bundled into a sack and plunged into darkness. He fought for a moment, but the fabric was rough and scraped against his feathers.

Bright light appeared from the opening of the sack and two firm hands lifted him out and placed him inside a small cage, one of many stacked along the floor in rows and columns, each holding a pigeon. Beside him, he heard a *pssst* noise.

"Francis, is that you?" another pigeon called. "Welcome home."

CHAPTER 17

FRANCIS

September 26, 1940

Even though he was finally home, for the first time in his life Francis felt lost. He wasn't sure what that word meant anymore: *home*. He'd always thought that it was the place you came from and the place you returned to, but now, inside his cramped, dusty cage, among dozens of other caged pigeons, he felt like a prisoner.

"It's been a while since we last saw you," a voice came from the cage next to his.

"Paddy, is that you?" Francis asked.

Paddy was a veteran; he'd been working as a carrier pigeon for longer than any other pigeon Francis had ever met. He was older than most of them, too—almost twelve—which in pigeon years was ancient. He still hadn't retired, though, not officially anyway. When the humans decided he was too old and too slow for them, they set him free. But he just kept on coming back, so they let him stay.

"Aye," Paddy replied. "It's been quiet around here with so many of the lads out on the front line."

Although he didn't say it outright, Francis could hear the sadness in Paddy's voice.

"Why do you stay here?" Francis asked. If Francis managed to make it to retirement, he knew that he wouldn't spend his last days in a dark, musty loft. He'd see the world, or as much of it as he could.

Paddy sighed. "I don't know, lad. I suppose I've got nowhere else to go. No purpose other than this."

"Couldn't you find a new purpose?"

"The National Pigeon Service is all I've ever known. There's nowhere else to go." He paused. "I wish I could have one last mission. One last adventure before my wings give up on me and the humans ditch me for good."

Francis examined the edges of his cage and the metal catch that secured the door shut. An idea began to form in his head of how he could warn his friends at the zoo and grant Paddy's wish at the same time.

"Paddy," Francis said, "I need your help." He raised his voice so that all the pigeons in the loft could hear him. "I've just delivered a message. The Nazis are planning to blitz London. The humans are preparing to defend the city and the humans in it, but what about the dogs and cats living on the streets, the birds, the pigeons living in Regent's Park...? What about the animals at the zoo? They don't have shelters to hide in or weapons to protect themselves with. They're not trained like we are. When the air-raid sirens sound and the Nazis attack, they don't stand a chance."

He felt something surge through his blood, through his very core. "We can save them. Or at least give them a chance to find somewhere safe to shelter."

"It's an honorable idea, Francis," Paddy said, "but why do you care about the zoo so much?"

"I was shot down," Francis said, and the loft suddenly went silent. Every pigeon there had a friend who had been lost to the war. But for one to have been hit and made it back alive—that was unheard of.

"What happened, lad?" Paddy asked.

"German bombers," Francis said. "Shot right through my wing. I thought that was it for me, but I landed in the zoo and the animals there...and the humans...they helped me. They saved my life. I owe them."

"What can we do?" Paddy asked, and a few others echoed the question.

"We need to warn them. It won't be much, but it will give them a little time, give them a fighting chance. Don't they deserve that?"

There was a deathly silence, apart from the odd shuffling sounds of feet scratching the floor. Francis sagged, the burden of needing to save his friends weighing heavy.

"I'm in," Paddy cried beside him.

"But the humans need us here," a voice said from above Francis. "Who will deliver their messages while we're gone?"

"They will be too busy with the incoming threat," Francis said. "Besides, we will only be gone a day. You all know that we can be here for days, weeks even, before being needed."

"It's too risky," said another.

"No riskier than what we do when we're at war," Francis said. "But now the war isn't far away in some foreign land. It's coming to us. To our home. To destroy everything and everyone."

A chorus of voices chattered and asked questions and argued among themselves while Francis tried to think of a better way to convince them.

"I'm in, too!" a voice shouted from the far side of the loft. "But how do we get out of our cages?"

A murmur rose as the others echoed this thought. Francis poked his beak through the wire mesh and gripped the metal catch with his beak. Slowly, slowly, he pulled, until with a small click, the door sprang open. He hopped out of his cage, then flew into the air so that the other pigeons could see him. Then he went to Paddy's cage and did the same, releasing him. Paddy moved to the left, while Francis moved to the right, repeating the action until every single pigeon was free.

"Who taught you how to do that?" Paddy asked as the pigeons assembled.

"A monkey." Francis grinned.

"The plan is simple," he told the crowd. "We fly to London and warn every animal we see. Tell them to warn everyone they know and to find somewhere safe. The humans won't let animals inside their shelters, but there's nothing to stop them from going into the underground train stations. They will be the safest places. If anyone doesn't want to come, that is your choice. I am asking you, as your friend, as your kin."

Francis waited for the pigeons to change their minds and return to their cages, but every single one stood firm, looking to him as their leader.

The pigeons bobbed their heads in unison, and Francis separated them into groups, assigning each group to a different area of the city.

"Red division, you'll take the east of the city. Frederick, you take the lead. Green division, the west, led by Bertha. Blue, north, led by Billy, and Yellow, south with Margaret." He nodded at a group of five pigeons in front of him. "The rest come with me to the center of London."

"What about me?" Paddy asked, disappointed to not have been put into a group.

"I've got a special job for you," Francis told him. "You and I are going to London Zoo. We've got some animals to save."

Francis took the lead and flew from the loft with Paddy by his side. The other pigeons flew behind in a V formation, flying over Bletchley Park Mansion like they were their very own air force. Someone spotted them from below and called out to the other humans, who rushed out of the huts, staring up at the sight of the pigeons flying as one.

"We'll be back!" Francis cooed to them.

Gradually, they reached the outer edges of the city. The sun was setting on the horizon, leaving nothing but a faint pink line. The sky was cloudless, and already stars dotted the indigo background.

Regent's Park was a few miles ahead and Francis's gut began to twist. He hadn't really thought much further than to escape and warn as many animals as he could. With the dogs and cats, it would be relatively simple. They could move about the city unseen. The zoo animals would be different. Their enclosures were not hardy enough to withstand any type of bomb, so there was no choice but to evacuate. But where could they go? Some of the smaller animals might be able to force their way into the zoo's basement shelter, but that was no option for the giraffes or zebras.

One thing at a time, Francis told himself. First, they would warn the animals and help them escape their enclosures, then after that, well, they would just have to cross that bridge when they came to it.

"Incoming!" Paddy shouted.

"Red division, dive!" Frederick ordered. He looked back at Francis and gave a quick nod before diving toward the ground.

"Yellow division, to the right," Francis yelled.

The pigeons peeled away from the main group, heading south.

The final groups quickly followed, each heading in a different direction, leaving Francis, Paddy, and his group on course as they headed to the center of the city.

"Nazi bombers," Francis replied as Messerschmitts appeared on the horizon. "We're too late!"

The air-raid sirens sounded below. Soon the streets were clear and eerily silent except for the echoing wail. Francis pushed harder, keeping the enemy within his sight. Something was different. The planes weren't in their usual formation of ten or twenty Messerschmitts.

Hundreds, maybe thousands of bomber planes peppered the sky like a swarm of locusts set to devour everything in their path.

It was the entire Luftwaffe.

CHAPTER 18

FRANCIS

September 26, 1940

They landed at the edge of the zoo. Francis directed the pigeons to spread out, then he moved from cage to cage, enclosure to enclosure.

"Something bad is coming!" he shouted as he went. "Get ready, we need to evacuate the zoo!"

The animals became increasingly distressed as the message traveled throughout the zoo. Questions were shouted at Francis as he went, until they merged into a jumble inside his head:

What is coming? What can we do? How do we get out of our cages?

"I'll be back," Francis reassured them as he ran past. "I'm breaking you out."

"Prepare to leave!" Francis shouted at the storks and ostriches.

They glared at him wide-eyed, then literally stuck their heads in the sand and refused to listen no matter how many times Francis shouted at them.

"We're ready!" the prairie dogs called, seemingly unperturbed by this new revelation. They lined up obediently at their cage door, nodding when Francis told them he'd be back.

There was a faint whistling sound as something fell from the sky, landing on the path ahead. It fizzed, then emitted a small flame. Francis stepped forward to take a closer look, but Paddy held him back.

"Incendiaries," he told Francis. "Watch out."

All around them, more and more incendiaries fell from the sky, raining down like droplets of fire. Some did nothing but fizz and hiss where they landed, but as one landed on the roof of a wooden shed nearby, Francis could see why they were so deadly. In an instant the roof ignited, and within minutes it was completely ablaze. The fire quickly spread to an overhanging tree branch and then to another tree, until the entire row was on fire.

The incendiaries continued to land on buildings and roofs, until it seemed like all of London was on fire. Francis left Paddy to continue preparing the animals, while he flew to Monkey Hill. As soon as the monkeys saw Francis, they crowded around, many of the younger monkeys clinging to their mothers' backs, their eyes wider than ever.

"Jacky, Chiney!" Francis called.

His friends appeared, giving Francis their usual grins, despite everything that was going on.

"I need your help." Francis coughed as smoke filled the air. "One last time."

"Anything," Chiney said.

"Just say the word," Jacky added.

"We're evacuating the zoo," Francis shouted so that the monkeys could hear. "As many animals as possible. I need you to unlock as many enclosures as you can, then we will find a safe place to shelter."

Paddy joined Francis and leaned over to whisper in his ear, "Are you sure you want to release *all* the animals?" He gestured to the lion enclosure, where two hungry-looking beasts stared back.

Francis looked at the lions. He didn't want to sentence them to death, but he couldn't risk the safety of the other animals and humans. The fires continued to rage all around them, and now, along with the incendiaries, bombs were being dropped. There were screams as humans ran for shelter. Their cries were drowned out by the echoing explosions and drones of planes—both enemies and allies—flying above. But worse than all of that was the sounds of the animals. Their terrified shrieks and screams rose above the noise as they realized there was danger of being bombed or trapped by fire.

"The humans made the zoo as secure as possible in case of a situation like this," Francis said finally as the air filled with black smoke. "They have reinforced shelters for the more dangerous animals, like the polar bears. The lions will be all right."

They have to be, he thought. He hoped he had made the right decision as the monkeys raced to unlock as many cages and enclosures as possible.

But now Francis had another problem. As animals gathered around him, he still had no idea where they could go. He strutted back and forth, desperately trying to find an answer when he walked smack bang into a wooden post. He shook his bruised head and looked up: It was the giant map of the zoo. He scanned it quickly, then his gaze fell upon the one place where they might all fit and have a chance of surviving the night.

"The east tunnel!" Francis shouted above the roar of the planes and the explosions that seemed to be going off every second. Even when he'd been stationed at Normandy, Francis had never seen war this up close before, and it terrified him.

As scared as he was, though, the other animals were petrified. Francis tried to tell them to calm down and make their way to the tunnel in groups so that they would be smaller targets. But instead, they stampeded—hippos, camels, and zebras, all running alongside monkeys and penguins and flamingoes. If the situation hadn't been so dire, Francis would have stopped just to take it all in—the sheer spectacle of so many different animals coming together as one.

"My foal!" a zebra cried, running over to Francis. "She's lost. Please help me find her!"

"Head to the tunnel," Francis told her. "I'll find her."

"What is going on!" a voice shrieked from behind him.

He turned to see Jean watching the escaped animals, her face smeared with black soot and her hands scratched up and bloodied.

Francis froze. Why was Jean there? She needed to be somewhere safe, away from the bombs. He flew over to her and she shook her head, unable to believe what she was seeing. "What is happening?" she screamed.

Francis hopped along the ground, trying to lead her toward the tunnel.

Jean gasped. "You're trying to get the animals to a shelter!"

She ran alongside Francis as he flew, shaking her head the whole way and muttering that he really was an amazing pigeon.

The east tunnel led from Regent's Park to the zoo and was long, made from concrete, with plenty of room to fit all the animals, and tall enough for the giraffes. Paddy led the way, while Francis stayed at the rear, ushering the animals inside. Jean was joined by a few other keepers who had come to find her, and together they herded the animals to safety, trying to calm them as best they could.

Francis landed beside Jean and she bent to stroke his head with shaking hands. "I'm scared," she whispered to him.

Francis bobbed his head, then he saw the zebra watching him anxiously.

"Paddy, I've got to go!" he called out. "There is a zebra foal out there somewhere."

He ignored Paddy's protests and flew out of the

tunnel, peering through the smoke for any sign of the lost foal.

A bomb exploded within the zoo grounds and a huge geyser of water burst forth from the ground as it hit the main water pipe. Francis fought against the heavy spray, but his wings were waterlogged. He ran instead, flapping his wings to dry them, when another bomb hit Monkey Hill.

Francis flew toward it, hoping that the monkeys had all evacuated. The concrete hill was a mess. A smoldering crater sizzled right in its center, and rock and debris had been flung far over the wall.

There was a slight movement from beneath one of the rocks, and a groan.

"Francis!" a small voice called.

Chiney!

Francis hurried over. His friend was trapped by the rock, his tail caught beneath it.

"What are you doing here?" Francis asked. "You should be in the tunnel."

"I came to help you," Chiney groaned.

"Stay still," Francis ordered. "I'll get you out of this."

He leaned his weight against the rock, but it was too heavy. He looked around desperately for someone to help, but the zoo was deserted.

He tried again, pushing with every ounce of strength he had left in him. Suddenly, it shifted. Paddy appeared beside him, pushing against the other side.

"You didn't think I'd leave you out here alone, did you, lad?" Paddy gasped as he pushed against the rock. Slowly, it scraped along the ground, until Chiney was able to pull his tail free.

"Are you all right?" Francis puffed. "I was so worried!"

Chiney gave him a shaky smile.

"Go to the tunnel," Francis ordered. "Make sure that everyone stays inside. You included."

Chiney didn't wait to be told twice; he raced off, disappearing into the arc of water.

"Come on!" Francis yelled to Paddy.

Paddy shook his head. "My wing," he said. "It's injured."

"Well, mine is, too," Francis said. "But I'm not going to let that stop us."

He wrapped his good wing around Paddy as the two hobbled along toward the tunnel. There was another explosion as the camel house was hit, blocking their path. Francis and Paddy were thrown back against a wall by the blast.

Francis gasped, trying to catch his breath and get his

bearings, searching for Paddy. A small bundle of bloodied feathers lay unmoving on the ground.

"Paddy?" Francis called, hurrying over to his friend.

Paddy groaned. "Pigeon down," he whispered.

Francis inspected his injuries. They were bad.

"It will be all right," Francis said. "Jean will help you. We'll shelter with the humans, and maybe they will let you stay here like I did. That would be a nice retirement for you, Paddy, wouldn't it? You'll like it here with all the animals. The visitors drop so much food, you'll be eating like a king. Paddy...?"

But Paddy could no longer hear him. Francis sagged beside his fallen friend, unable to move, unable to think.

"I'm sorry," Francis cried. "I'm so, so sorry."

Francis didn't know how long he stayed beside his friend, but he suddenly became aware of fire licking the trees around him. It scorched his feathers, and smoke filled his lungs. A little way ahead, he saw the outline of the restaurant. As much as he wanted to stay by Paddy's side, Francis had made Ming a promise. He wasn't going to break it.

He flew low toward the restaurant, trying to find somewhere to shelter. He hoped that there would be a door or window ajar to squeeze through, but a shower of fireballs whizzed through the air, landing on the restaurant's roof. He flew on, up and over the restaurant, swerving this way and that to avoid the incoming missiles. Finally, he saw the tunnel up ahead.

Chiney and Jacky peered out from the entrance, anxiously searching the sky.

"I'm here," Francis puffed as he landed. The zebra came rushing forward, but Francis shook his head. "I couldn't find her," he said. "I'm sorry."

"We thought we'd never see you again," Jacky said, hugging Francis.

"Thank you for saving my life," Chiney said quietly.

Francis sobbed. "That was all Paddy's doing."

"Where is he?" Chiney looked past Francis, but when Francis lowered his head, Chiney knew that Paddy wouldn't be joining them.

Deep in the tunnel, the animals waited in silence. They listened as the bombs exploded around the city and sirens wailed. Gunfire echoed through the tunnel, the sound amplified so that it was even louder inside than out.

Francis rested against the wall, and Jean took him in her arms and hugged him close. There was nothing more to do but hope that the other pigeons were safe and that the tunnel wouldn't be hit.

CHAPTER 19
MING

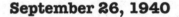

September 26, 1940

The wolves knew something was wrong before the humans did. Their desperate howls were loud and urgent and incessant. The sirens started, and the two sounds intertwined into one long, mournful wail.

The other animals in the zoo began crying out, the elephants trumpeting in fear. They weren't as used to the air raids as Ming and Tang had become—the half-a-breath pause before the blast, the bright flashes of light, the heat from the fire warming the night air, and the smoke that brought with it a lingering smell that sometimes lasted for days.

Ming looked in the direction of the wolves' howls. Waiting to see what was coming. Suddenly, she had her answer as planes flew overhead, not from the direction that Ming had expected, but from behind, startling her so much that she jumped higher than a baby kangaroo.

"Is it an attack?" Sung asked, her voice wobbling.

Ming surveyed the bombers as they flew by. "I don't think so," she answered. "Do you see the markings on the planes?"

Sung narrowed her eyes, then nodded.

"The planes with circles beneath their wings and on the tail are British," she explained. "That means they are on our side."

"What about the enemy?" Sung asked. "What do their planes look like?"

"They have black crosses," Tang piped up.

"I didn't think you paid much attention to Francis!" Ming exclaimed, surprised.

Tang shrugged. "Francis is my friend, too."

Another squadron of Spitfires flew over, but one lagged behind the others. Black smoke trailed from the engine, and it sputtered through the air, the propellers stalling before restarting again. It roared back to life, speeding ahead to catch up with the others, but something fell from its undercarriage.

Before Ming could shout out a warning, the bomb

landed just beyond the giraffes' paddock. She threw herself at Tang and Sung and knocked them to the ground, sacrificing her own safety to shield them with her body. Ming felt as though she were caught inside a firestorm. The explosion sent a fierce blast sweeping over them in scorching waves. She held her paws over her head as she heard the giraffes' screams and the wolves howls far in the distance.

The humans arrived quickly, dunking buckets into the pond to douse the flames. The bomb hadn't destroyed any buildings, but half of the strawberry patch in the field was now a smoldering black crater. In the paddock, zookeepers were trying to keep the giraffes calm, but the baby seemed especially agitated. There was another small blast far in the distance, and the baby giraffe set off at an incredible pace, almost trampling the men fighting the fire.

Some of the humans, still wearing their bathrobes, raced after the giraffe as she ran through the wooden fence, knocking it down, and continued on until Ming could no longer see her. Ming tried to move, but her limbs were weak and trembling.

"We...have...to help!" Ming managed, coughing up dust and soot.

Tang murmured in reply, but Ming, her ears ringing, couldn't hear him.

"Get off!" Tang shouted, elbowing Ming so that she would get the message.

Ming groaned and forced herself up while Tang did the same, checking himself and Ming over for any injuries. They both seemed in good shape, surprisingly. Sung, however, sat in silence, staring off into space. The dancing glow of the fire reflected in her eyes.

"We have to help," Ming repeated.

The blast had created a hole in one side of the wire-mesh fence surrounding their enclosure. Ming tentatively stepped closer to examine it. The edges were twisted and jagged. Sharp pieces jutted out at different angles, but it was big enough, Ming thought, for a giant panda to fit through if she wanted to escape. She turned to Sung, who sat looking up at the sky. Tang sat beside her, trying to break her out of it. The planes had long since disappeared. The sky seemed clear again, and Ming could no longer hear the drone of propellers or plane engines.

"Are you coming?" Ming asked, trying to keep her voice steady.

Tang glanced up at her and shook his head vigorously, gesturing to Sung, but Ming persisted.

"Sung?" she asked.

"What are you doing?" Tang asked. "You can't go out there."

"Francis would have helped the other animals," Ming said. "I think we should, too."

She eased her way through the hole in the wire mesh and glanced around. The humans were preoccupied with the giraffes. Farther along the path, a storage shed had been knocked down by the blast.

"Do you hear that?" Tang asked from beside her.

"You came!" Ming smiled.

"Well, why should you and Francis be the only heroic ones?" Tang shrugged.

A small squealing noise came from the dilapidated shed. *It is little more than a wooden shack*, Ming thought. No wonder it had been destroyed.

They ventured slowly toward the wreckage, picking their way carefully across the debris and shattered wooden boards. There was a slight movement from beneath the pile of lumber.

"Look!" Ming gasped. A small hand reached out from beneath the pile. "It's a human child."

She used her paws to carefully pull the timber boards aside. "Help me, Tang!"

Tang joined her, using his jaws to pick up smaller pieces.

"Be careful," Ming warned. "We don't want to hurt her."

"Mama!" the small voice called.

"We'll have you out of there soon, little human," Ming shushed. "Try to stay calm."

Tang stared at Ming for a moment. "Who are you and what have you done with Ming?" he asked.

Ming pulled away another large plank of wood. "What do you mean?" she asked.

"You wouldn't even leave the shadows to see the humans," he replied, "and now..."

Ming sighed. "Things change," she said. "This war...it changes you. But I am glad it has brought us closer. That we are friends."

Tang smiled, and the two increased their efforts to free the little girl.

Finally, she escaped. Her face was filthy, covered in scratches and scrapes, and her white nightdress was torn, but she seemed to be able to move easily now that she was no longer trapped beneath the rubble.

The little girl brushed down her dress, then looked at the pandas in awe. "Thank you!" she whispered before running off toward the humans.

"We'd better check on Sung," Ming said, hurrying back to their ruined enclosure.

Sung was much the same as when they'd left her. "She's shell-shocked," Tang said. "It's what the humans say when someone has had a traumatic experience."

"Well, we'll have to snap her out if it," Ming said. "Sung, I thought I might head up to the pavilion, take a look at that wonderful view you told me about. Wouldn't you like to see it?"

Sung slowly slid her gaze from the sky to Ming, then gave the slightest of nods.

"Ming, I don't think this is a good idea," Tang hissed. "She's trembling all over. Look at her!"

"I can see that!" Ming hissed back. "Which is why she needs something to distract her from what just happened. You should come, too," she told him. "A bit of exercise will do you good. You look much rounder than when we first arrived."

The challenge worked; Tang forgot all about changing Ming's mind and instead followed after her and Sung, grumbling as they carefully eased their way through the torn wire mesh, sneaked past the humans, and plodded up the hill. It was steeper than Ming had thought and the summit farther away than it seemed. They eventually reached the top, huffing and puffing as they tried to catch their breath.

The view was stunning. The full moon cast a light over the vast countryside that spread out before them, like a spotlight illuminating a stage. There was a forest of tall, dark trees to the west, and fields and hills as far as the eye could see to the very horizon. Ming narrowed her eyes, focusing on a blurred orange glow at the center of the horizon.

"What's over there?" she asked Sung, who sat beside her.

Sung followed Ming's gaze, then stood so suddenly that Ming's stomach lurched.

"What is it?" Ming whispered. Sung's eyes had grown wide, and her fur trembled again.

"I told you this was a bad idea," Tang said. He patted Sung's shoulder gently with a paw, but she flinched.

"I'm so sorry," Sung whispered.

"Sorry?" Ming asked, confused. "About what?"

Sung gestured at the glowing blur, which seemed to have grown bigger and brighter in the fleeting moments that Ming had looked away.

Ming's heart pounded in her chest, spreading a sickening feeling of unease through her body. "What is it, Sung?" she cried, unable to take the tension any longer.

"London," Sung told her.

Tang's jaw grew slack as he stared at the glow lighting up the sky so many, many miles away. "It looks like the sky is on fire," he whispered.

Ming couldn't understand what was happening. She heard the words, but they made no sense. When they had left the zoo, London, everything had been fine. The nightly air raids were terrifying but they got through them. They survived. But now...now her world was slowly unraveling around her. Everything she had ever known...the zoo...her friends...her home. Could it really all be gone? Had Francis been too late delivering his message?

Sung gripped Ming tightly with her paw. "London is burning."

CHAPTER 20

FRANCIS

September 27, 1940

The restaurant was still burning. The burst pipe continued to spurt out water, creating a meandering river that wound its way through the zoo. The firefighters had been forced to use the only other supply of water at the zoo, which was the sea lion pool. The sea lions stood around, watching the humans with varying degrees of emotion on their faces, ranging from mild annoyance to pure rage that their pool was being drained.

Francis heard them complaining as he wandered past, being careful to avoid the humans. At least water was the only thing they had lost, he thought bitterly. The water main could be fixed, the pool refilled. But nothing could bring back Paddy.

When the air raid had subsided and the humans began emerging from their shelters to inspect the damage, Francis had told the animals to return to their enclosures—those who had enclosures to return to. A few animals still wandered the zoo, looking as dazed and exhausted as Francis felt.

The camel house had been badly damaged, so they stood aimlessly in a nearby paddock, staring at one another as though wondering what to do next. As Francis headed toward Monkey Hill, there were many more disoriented animals. Francis had seen humans with the same lost expressions at Normandy—those who had returned from the front line, some injured, some worse, with their eyes glazed over. It was as though the war and what they had been through had erased some part of them, destroyed all sense of what was right and what was wrong. Their minds filled with the horrors they had seen, the images replaying over and over while they wondered what they should have done differently. Why their comrades and friends didn't make it.

Francis knew all this because he felt the same way now. It was an aching pain that he didn't think would ever go away. He'd wanted to give Paddy one last adventure, one final mission so that he could retire with a sense of peace. But now he would never have that. All that Francis had given his old friend was pain. He hoped that the other pigeons had made their way back to Bletchley. He couldn't bear to think that more of them might have been hurt because of him.

Ahead, a group of humans had a zebra surrounded, trying to coax her toward a large wooden outhouse, but she was having none of it. She brayed and kicked out, narrowly missing the leg of one of the keepers, who cursed out loud. The zebra had gone to the zebra house in the hope that her foal might have returned there during the night, but it was clear that nothing was inside. The roof had collapsed, and the building had been blasted to bits.

"The foal is under the hippo!" one of the female keepers called out, running across the paddock toward them.

Francis smiled despite himself. Hippos were the stockiest, toughest beasts he had ever seen. Hiding beneath one would be a clever, if not slightly dangerous, move. The zebra calmed down upon hearing that her foal was safe and allowed herself to be led to the outhouse along with the other zebras.

The monkeys, despite their hill having been blown to smithereens, seemed the least affected by the night's events. Francis watched them in awe, wishing he had their resilience. The smaller monkeys leaped and bounded over the rubble, whooping and sliding into the giant crater, enjoying the new configuration. The sight of their joy gave Francis a little hope that maybe, one day, he could feel that kind of happiness once again.

Jacky and Chiney stood atop a boulder and waved. Francis bobbed his head in reply, but he had no time to stay and chat. He had one final promise to keep. He flew over to the giant panda enclosure, relieved to see that it was still intact. Although Ming and Tang were no longer there, he would have been sad to have seen it destroyed.

He made his way to the back of the enclosure, where he found Jean, sobbing quietly to herself. Francis hopped onto a branch and cooed at her softly. Jean looked up, wiping the back of her hand across her face.

"Hello," she whispered hoarsely, trying to give Francis a small smile but failing miserably. The sight of him seemed to set her off again, and she held her face in her hands, snuffling.

"It's so awful," she sobbed. "The zoo...it's just..." She couldn't finish her sentence, but she didn't need to. Francis understood.

"Jean?" a quiet voice called.

Jean wiped her tears away. "Here."

Another zookeeper came into the enclosure. "Oh, Jean," she cried, pulling Jean into a hug. "Are you all right? We were so worried about you when you and the others went missing last night. The boss was going out of his mind with worry."

Jean gulped, then nodded. "I'm sorry," she said. "I didn't mean to worry you all. I just couldn't leave the animals."

"That was a brave thing you did," the other zookeeper said. "Reckless, but brave. Whatever gave you the idea to take them to the tunnel?"

Jean gave Francis a small smile. "A little bird told me."

The zookeeper frowned, then pulled a piece of paper from her pocket. "A telegram arrived for the boss from Whipsnade. Have you seen him?"

"No," Jean sniffled. "I can give it to him, though."

"I think you'd better. He needs to know you're safe."

The zookeeper handed Jean the telegram, then gave her one last hug before leaving Jean and Francis alone.

She unfolded the paper and read it, her face turning white.

She gasped and stared at Francis. "Whipsnade!" she cried. "It was hit by a bomb last night!"

Francis felt the ground move beneath him. *Ming. Tang.* He should have gone to Whipsnade first. He should have warned them, too!

Jean wailed and began crying even harder. Francis wanted to stay and comfort her, but he couldn't. He set off at once, soaring over London. Below him, in the early morning light, fires continued to rage on. The humans were still fighting them, despite the devastation. Entire buildings that had once stood tall and proud were now nothing put piles of blackened rubble and ash. The humans searched through the remains of their homes, their lives.

But the Nazis hadn't succeeded in destroying one thing that still rose proudly in the center of London: Despite being surrounded by fires, Saint Paul's Cathedral was miraculously untouched. It was a symbol that no matter how hard the enemy tried to defeat London, Britain remained strong. Its great dome shone in the sunlight like a beacon of hope, and Francis flew faster, spurred on by the thought that if such a building could make it through the blitz untouched, then perhaps his friends could, too.

CHAPTER 21
MING

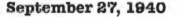

"Where are you going?" Tang demanded as Ming set off down the hill in the direction of the hideous glowing light in the distance. Dark black clouds gathered overhead ominously.

"Home!" Ming replied breathlessly. "I need to know if our friends are all right. If Jean and Jacky and Chiney and all the others…" She paused. She couldn't say any more. She wouldn't. She wasn't going to let herself even consider the possibility that those she loved might be injured or worse. At least Francis was safe at Bletchley.

She reached the bottom of the hill and half ran, half stumbled into the woods, crashing through the trees like a lumbering elephant, and just as noisy.

"Come back!" Tang called, struggling to keep up.

Ming was amazed how fast she could actually move when she set her mind to it.

"You don't have to come with me," she called back. "Stay with Sung."

She heard Tang pause, and for a moment her heart squeezed inside her chest. She wanted to do this. She was *going* to do this. But having Tang by her side would have made it a little less scary.

Tang appeared beside her. "Do you even know where you're going?"

Ming gave him a grateful smile. "Toward the glow," she said. "To London."

Tang stared at her as though it was taking every ounce of his energy not to argue, but to Ming's surprise, he kept his mouth shut. They continued on in silence. The woods were full of creeping shadows and creaking sounds, and Ming tried not to think of what might be watching them. Instead, she imagined she was back at home in China, wandering through the bamboo forests, when everything was safe and she had no worries. *And no friends*, she thought suddenly.

She hadn't had any friends until Francis and Tang and Sung and the monkeys.

She hurried on, determined to return to her friends. It might well take her days...weeks even, but she would make sure they were all right and find Francis. Then she would go back to her enclosure with Tang and Jean and never let anyone take them away from her ever again.

The trees grew thicker and closer together. Their twisting trunks and branches blocked the way. Ming turned back, frustrated, and Tang followed silently, until after the fifth time they'd turned to go in the opposite direction.

"We are lost!" he cried, throwing his paws into the air. "I told you this was a bad idea, Ming. What is the plan? To wander aimlessly in the woods forever until we die or get eaten?"

He shuddered as a wolf howled not too far off in the distance.

Ming tried to remain calm. "We will find the way," she said. "Giant pandas live in the forest. We must have some natural instincts to ensure that we won't get lost."

"Ming!" Tang huffed. "We are not the same as wild giant pandas anymore. We grew up in a zoo in Britain, not in the wilds of China, and we are not Francis, either. We don't have a natural homing instinct that is miraculously going to kick in."

At the mention of Francis's name, Ming felt her resolve and any confidence she'd had in herself dissipate. "I have to do *something*, Tang!" she cried. "Francis said that to overcome fear, you have to do what scares you. You have to do what's right. What your heart tells you to do."

All her courage suddenly left her as all the terrible things that had happened hit her all at once. She sat down, defeated. "I want to go home," she said in a small voice.

Tang sat beside her. "Me too," he said. "But this is not the way. We'll never make it to London, no matter how determined you are."

There was another howl, and Ming froze. Her fur rose as she sensed a new creature close by. A predator.

"Tang," she started, but he shushed her.

He stood and moved in a slow circle around Ming, protecting her within it, peering through the trees for any signs of life.

"What is it?" Ming squeaked, trembling.

Tang backed up suddenly, and Ming stood beside him, coming face-to-face with a very large gray wolf. She turned to flee, but two more wolves joined the first, then another and another until the pandas were surrounded.

"Tang!" Ming squeaked again. "What are the wolves doing out here?"

"They must have escaped their enclosure," he hissed. "Try to stay calm."

The wolves continued to glare silently. This was their natural territory, and Ming and Tang were intruders.

Something fluttered above, and Ming broke eye contact with the wolf, glancing up. She didn't know what had made her do it, especially considering the situation she was in, but it was as though she was meant to see what was above. Suddenly, she didn't care that she was lost in the woods surrounded by a pack of fierce wolves who were probably half-starved. All she cared about was that she could see *him*.

"Francis!" she cried as he flew overhead. Somehow, impossibly, he was there. "I'm here! Francis!"

But Francis hadn't heard her. Hadn't seen her. He seemed so intent on his destination that his eyes were set straight ahead.

"Francis!" Tang joined in with Ming's desperate calls.

Ming looked to the wolves, who watched curiously. "*Please*, help us!" she begged. "That's our friend. He needs to know that we are safe."

The wolf at the front of the pack nodded almost imperceptibly. Then he raced after Francis with the pack chasing behind, moving swiftly but silently through the trees. Ming and Tang followed as fast as they could until they reached a small clearing. The wolves made a circle then, as one, lifted their heads to the sky and howled, so loud and for so long that Ming thought they must have been heard all the way to London and back again.

CHAPTER 22

FRANCIS

September 27, 1940

Francis had never flown so fast in his life. His wings seemed to have taken on a life of their own, as if they knew what he had to do and were making up for all the times they had failed him in the past. Francis's mind was empty but for one thought: *Find Ming and Tang.*

Nothing else mattered now. The war, the National Pigeon Service, Bletchley. All that mattered was making sure that Ming and Tang were safe.

Heavy clouds rolled in, darkening the sky as he soared over undulating hills and fields and vast woodland stretching for miles. He flew on, swooping low above the canopy of trees, oaks and birch and chestnut, until Whipsnade came into view atop a tall hill.

He was almost there when a long, painful cry called to him from below.

Wolves.

He flew on, slightly shaken by the unusual sound, when it came again, louder this time, and beneath it, something else—a whisper on the wind that almost sounded like someone calling his name.

Ming!

Francis turned, following the wolves' siren call. He had no idea why or how Ming had found herself in the woods, but he knew she was there, as surely as he knew his own name.

He swooped down to land, faltering when he saw the circle of wolves. They turned to look at him as one, then backed away, vanishing into the trees in the blink of an eye, leaving two giant pandas standing alone in the middle of the forest, looking impossibly out of place.

"Francis!" Ming shouted, lumbering over to him.

Tang gave Francis a wide smile, looking almost as pleased to see him as Ming was.

"Thank heaven!" Tang breathed. "Finally! Someone who can help us find the way home."

Francis smiled at him, then turned to Ming, his chest feeling a little less tight, his heart feeling a little less lost.

"You're alive!" he whispered.

Ming nodded, unable to speak. Then she grabbed him in a tight hug, until Tang had to remind her that pigeons were delicate creatures and she was likely crushing him to death.

Francis nodded to Tang gratefully when Ming finally released him.

"The zoo," Ming said quietly. "What happened?"

"The Luftwaffe came, as the message said they would," Francis told them. "I left Bletchley as soon as I heard. I tried to warn as many animals as I could, but…" He trailed off. "The zoo was badly hit; my friend, Paddy…didn't make it."

Ming's eyes sparkled with tears.

"Jean?" Tang asked. "And the monkeys?"

"They are all right," Francis said, relieved he had some good news to tell them. "But the war is far from over," he warned. "The Nazis will return. They will send more planes and more fighters. But we will continue to fight back until we win this war."

"Does that mean you are going back to Bletchley?" Ming asked.

Francis lowered his head. "I have to," he said. "At least until the war is over."

"I understand," Ming replied. "I'm very proud of you, Francis."

Tang cleared his throat beside them. "Perhaps, before Francis sets off on another important mission, he could show us the way back to the zoo? As helpful as those wolves were, I'm not sure I particularly want to see them again."

MING

May 8, 1945

Ming and Tang lay out in the midafternoon sun, enjoying the attention from the crowds. "Look, there's another one!" Tang called out as he spotted a small boy clutching one of the zoo's newest additions to the gift shop—a Tang toy.

"That's the seventh one I've seen today," he boasted. "I think they are becoming more popular than the Mings."

Ming smiled, letting him savor the moment. She didn't have the heart to tell him that the Tang toys were exactly the same as the Mings apart from the fact that they were labeled differently.

The crowd was one of the biggest that Ming had ever seen. Most children had come home to London, and many men—those who could—had also returned. A buzz of excitement and anticipation filled the air, as though everyone was waiting for something to happen. Ming wasn't sure what it was, but she found that she was actually enjoying the attention for once.

"Shall we try out our new trick?" she asked Tang.

The monkeys had been teaching them ways to improve their performance. The pandas had failed terribly at leaping, and after Ming landed on her head attempting a somersault, she had decided against trying out any more acrobatics. Eventually, though, the monkeys had found something that the giant pandas were actually capable of.

"I will if you will," Tang said with a grin.

They walked up onto their platform and stood in the center, waiting for the crowd to hush. Then they each turned to face the walkway back down and leaned forward, rolling headfirst to the ground.

Ming landed on the ground in a heap, but it didn't matter—the crowd went wild, clapping and hooting and chanting their names.

"Maybe we could try it backward next time?" Tang suggested.

Jean came running out from the back of the enclosure,

holding up her small wireless radio. She shouted at the crowd to be quiet, and a hush descended as a small, tinny voice came over the speaker.

It was the prime minister, Winston Churchill. Ming couldn't catch all of what he was saying because the sound was fuzzy and the crowd kept murmuring anxiously. But he spoke of the resilience of the people and never giving up.

There was more after that, but Ming could hear no more as the entire zoo erupted in cheers and chants. Men and women hugged, pulling their children tightly to them as tears streamed down their faces, and all across London shouts of *Victory!* and *War is over!* could be heard.

Ming looked at Tang, her eyes shining and her heart full of a strange mixture of joy and sadness that she'd never known before "It's over, Tang!" she cried. "It's really over!"

Tang smiled at her and nudged his head against her shoulder affectionately. Ming paused for a moment, then grinned back, nudging him just a little bit harder than he'd nudged her. Then she left the humans to their revelry, retiring once more to the shadows of her enclosure.

"Are you all right?" a voice said beside her.

"Francis!" Ming jumped up to greet her old friend. "It's been so long! I was worried that..." She didn't have to say any more; he knew what she meant.

"Why the sad face?" Francis asked her. "The war is over."

Ming thought of the advice Francis had given her all those years ago, and she took a breath to chase away her fears and sadness.

"I'm glad," she said. "Of course I am. But I can't help thinking of all those lives that were lost. Humans and animals. So much of the world destroyed, so many lives to rebuild." She took another breath as all the emotions—relief, joy, sadness, the fear that it might not be true, that the war wasn't really over—welled up inside her, catching in her throat.

Francis bobbed his head in a nod. "Hopefully," he said, "the world will have learned something from this tragedy. That is the one good thing that could come of it."

"Jean!" the boss yelled.

Ming and Francis jumped, fear clutching Ming's chest. He hauled the enclosure door open, searching for Jean, his gaze pausing as he saw Francis sitting in plain view. But instead of berating Francis or Jean, the boss simply smiled. "Even you can't ruin this wondrous day for me, pigeon!" he boomed.

"Father!"

The boss turned and hugged his daughter, and Ming was surprised to see that he, too, had tears in his eyes.

Francis settled down beside Ming in his usual spot on top of the straw.

"Does this mean that you can stay for a while?" Ming asked.

"I've decided to retire from the National Pigeon Service," he replied. "Let some other young pigeon have the adventures for a change."

Ming smiled, and Tang came to join them, the three friends watching as the humans celebrated. She liked to think that the zoo and its inhabitants reflected the humans' struggles: they, too, were evacuated, their food rationed, and they, too, lost their homes and their loved ones. She had heard some of the humans call it the "people's war," but to Ming, Francis, and all the others, it would always be known as their war. A struggle fought and overcome not just by the humans, but by the animals, too.

Author's Note

Francis and Ming's story is set during what became known as the Battle of Britain and the Blitz. But this battle waged against London by Nazi Germany was only a small part of World War II and just one of thousands of battles that were fought all across the world. Almost every country in the world became involved in the war in some way. Many joined the side of the Axis powers, which included most notably Germany, Japan, and Italy; others joined the side of the Allies, which included Great Britain, France, Canada, the United States, China, and the Soviet Union.

The war lasted six years, from 1939 to 1945, and many cities and towns were destroyed during that time, and many lives were lost. In less fortunate countries and rural areas, there were no armies, navy, or air force to come to the rescue when under attack or invaded. Until the Allies came to their aid, they had no one but themselves to stand up and fight for their homes and their lives. In Great Britain and around the world, many animals lost their lives, too, not only those caught in air raids, bombings, and fires, but when food was rationed, there was less to eat for everyone, including family pets; many were set free to fend for themselves.

At Whipsnade Zoo, land was put aside for farming so that the zoo could feed both human and animal inhabitants, providing food for the animals at London Zoo that had otherwise been imported from abroad. The craters left behind by bombs hitting land at Whipsnade and then being turned into ponds also actually happened. With many of the men away at war, it became too much work to fill in the craters.

Bletchley Park played a big role during the war. It was the central site for the Allied forces code breakers and was where intelligence officers were able to hack into and decode information about the Axis powers' movements. This enabled the Allies to stay one step ahead at times and to prevent attacks before the enemy reached their intended targets, preventing the loss of many more lives. It has even been said that the work done at Bletchley shortened the length of the war by two years, as without the vital information the code breakers were able to procure, the Germans and Axis powers would have certainly invaded more countries and been more successful in their attacks.

In this book, Francis is able to alert those in power of the Nazis' plans to blitz London so that the Royal Air Force could respond in time. In real life, there were many pigeons like Francis who risked their lives along with the human soldiers to get important messages where they needed to go, and so they, too, had a part in helping to end what was, hopefully, the last world war our planet will ever see.

SURVIVAL TAILS

TAILS

WORLD WAR II

FACT FILE

Animals at London Zoo

London Zoo opened in 1828 and is still a thriving zoo today at the heart of Regent's Park in London. It houses more than twenty thousand animals and over seven hundred different species, including endangered species such as pygmy hippos, pangolins, tigers, and Asian elephants.

Through the years, it has been home to many special animals, some who became famous and much-loved, such as Ming. A black bear called Winnie lived at the zoo at the beginning of the First World War. It was then that the author of the classic Winnie-the-Pooh stories, A. A. Milne, visited the zoo with his son and inspiration struck.

A gorilla named Guy lived at the zoo from 1947 to 1978, and there is now a statue in his honor. Apparently

Guy was a bird lover and used to gently pick up small birds that entered his enclosure and then release them.

In 1865 an elephant named Jumbo was brought to London Zoo. He was trained by zookeepers and would give visitors rides around the park. The zoo also housed animals that are sadly now extinct, such as the quagga, which looked similar to a zebra and was hunted to extinction, and the thylacine, also known as a Tasmanian tiger, which looked similar to a striped wolf or dog with a long, thin tail.

Jacky and Chiney were named after chimpanzees who lived at London Zoo during World War II. Monkey Hill was hit by a bomb, as depicted in this book, but there were no casualties. Rather than try to capture the monkeys, the zookeepers waited for them to return for food, which they eventually did.

The zebra house received a direct hit from the bombing during the Blitz, and miraculously none of the animals were harmed. They had somehow managed to escape alive. I like to think, as I have imagined in this book, they had a bit of help from some friends!

The zoo provided visitors the opportunity to see animals that Londoners had never seen before, which is why animals such as Ming the giant panda became so popular and well loved.

Animal Facts

GIANT PANDAS

- The giant panda, also known simply as panda, lives in the bamboo forests of Central China.

- Although they do eat meat and fish, their diet consists almost entirely of bamboo shoots and leaves.

- They usually live for around twenty years and can weigh up to 285 pounds!

PIGEONS

- Baby pigeons are known as squabs and are ready to leave the nest when they are around two months old.

- Pigeons can fly up to seven hundred miles in a single day and at speeds of up to ninety miles per hour.

- They have extraordinary navigating abilities, and it doesn't matter how far they fly, they can almost always find their way back home.

SQUIRREL MONKEYS

- Although the squirrel monkey is one of the smallest monkeys, it is considered to be one of the smartest.

- They are found in South America and eat fruit and insects.

- They love company and usually live in very large groups, often with up to hundreds in a single group.

The Blitz

The Blitz, or blitzkreig as it was called by the Germans, means "lightning war." During World War II, the Blitz attack on Great Britain started during the Battle of Britain. The Germans had begun a series of air raids on Great Britain in 1940, starting with ports, industrial cities, and factories. Anything that might weaken Britain and also show that the Luftwaffe—the German air force—was superior to the British Royal Air Force—the RAF. But after the RAF proved to be the stronger force, Adolf Hitler set in motion Operation Sea Lion, an all-out attack on London, its civilians and populated areas, intending to bring the capital to its knees.

From September 7, the Luftwaffe bombed London

both night and day for a continued period of fifty-seven days, during which much of London was destroyed. People took to their air-raid shelters in their gardens or below their houses, and those who had no shelter of their own fled to the underground stations to take refuge from the continuous onslaught of bombs. The assault on London finally ended in May 1941 when German soldiers were sent to invade Russia. When the Luftwaffe failed, they began to bomb the ports to hit navy resources and industrial cities in an attempt to hurt Britain in a different way.

In the first night of the Blitz, over two thousand civilians were either killed or injured. Hitler intended to break the morale of the British people, but he failed. One example during the Blitz was when the Nazis targeted Saint Paul's Cathedral in the center of London. Despite the Nazis' best efforts and much of London burning to the ground around the cathedral, firefighters and civilians alike worked together to save the famous cathedral and its dome. And at the end of the Blitz, many evacuees returned home, and London, like many other cities and villages affected by the war, began rebuilding the city.

World War II Time Line

1939

September 1: The Second World War starts in Europe when Germany invades Poland.

September 3: France and Britain declare war on Germany. Those countries fighting alongside the United Kingdom and France are known as the Allies. Australia and New Zealand also join the Allies against Germany.

September 5: The United States declares that they will not be taking sides and would remain neutral at this point in the war.

September 6: South Africa declares war on Germany.

September 10: Canada declares war on Germany.

September 17: The Soviet Union joins Germany in

invading Poland, becoming known as the Axis powers working against the Allies.

September 19: The Japanese Imperial Army attacks the Chinese Revolutionary Army.

November 30: The Soviet Union invades Finland.

1940

April 9: Germany invades Norway and Denmark. Both countries eventually surrender to Germany.

May 10: Winston Churchill becomes the new prime minister of Britain after Neville Chamberlain resigns.

May 12: German forces enter France.

May 26: Around 340,000 British, French, and Belgian soldiers are evacuated from the beaches of Dunkirk in the north of France.

June 10: Italy enters the war against Britain and France, joining the Axis powers.

June 14: Germany invades Paris and takes control.

July 10: Germany launches nightly air attacks on Great Britain. These attacks last until the end of October and are known as the Battle of Britain.

September 7: The German blitz on London starts and doesn't end until May 1941.

September 27: Germany, Italy, and Japan sign the Tripartite Pact, creating the Axis Alliance.

October 28: Italy invades Greece.

November: Hungary, Romania, and Slovakia join Germany and the Axis powers.

1941

March 1: Bulgaria joins the Axis powers.

April 6: Germany invades Greece and Yugoslavia.

June 22: Germany and the Axis powers attack Russia.

December 7: Japan attacks the US Navy in Pearl Harbor.

December 8: The United States declares war on Japan and joins World War II on the side of the Allies.

December 11: Germany and Italy declare war on the United States, and the US responds accordingly.

1942

February: Japan invades and takes control of Singapore.

June 4: The US Navy defeats the Japanese Imperial Navy in the Battle of Midway, fought close to Hawaii.

August: The Allies enter North Africa, where they fight against the Germans and Italians.

August 23: The Battle of Stalingrad begins in Russia.

Germany and the Axis powers fight for control of the Russian city.

1943
February 2: The Germans surrender to the Soviet Union after the defeat in Stalingrad.
May 13: In North Africa, the Axis forces surrender to the Allies.
May 16: RAF forces attack German dams, known as the Dambusters Raid.
September 8: Italy surrenders and changes sides to join the Allies, weakening the Axis powers significantly.

1944
June 6: D-Day and the Normandy Invasion. Allied forces invade France and push back the Germans.
August 25: Paris is liberated from German control.
December 16: The Germans launch the final large attack in the Battle of the Bulge. They eventually lose to the Allies.

1945
February 19: US Marines invade the Japanese island of Iwo Jima and eventually capture the island.

April 12: US President Franklin Roosevelt dies. He is succeeded by President Harry Truman.

April 30: Adolf Hitler commits suicide, as he knows Germany has lost the war.

May 7: Germany surrenders to the Allies, ending the war in Europe.

August 6: The United States drops the atomic bomb on Hiroshima, Japan. The city is devastated.

August 9: Another atomic bomb is dropped on Nagasaki, Japan.

September 2: Japan surrenders to US General Douglas MacArthur and the Allies. The war is over.

Glossary

AIR RAID: an assault from the sky, usually with bombs

AIR-RAID SIREN: a loud siren that warns large populations of approaching danger

ALLIES: a person, group, or country with a common cause

BARRAGE BALLOON: a large balloon anchored near or around a city with large wires, used as a defense from low-flying planes

BLETCHLEY PARK: the code-breaking facility in Britain

BLITZKRIEG: in German means "lightning war," an intensive bombing often from the sky

BLITZ: shortened version of blitzkrieg

CODE BREAKER: a person who deciphers codes, working at a facility such as Bletchley Park

ENLIST: to join or enroll in something, often military service

EVACUATE: to leave a place, often due to potential danger

HOME GUARD: a volunteer force for when the army is located somewhere else

INCENDIARIES: bombs used to set things on fire

LIEUTENANT GENERAL: a high-ranking officer in the army

LUFTWAFFE: the German air force

MESSERSCHMITT: bomber plane used by the German air force

NAZI: a member of the National Socialist German Workers' Party, led by Adolf Hitler during the Second World War

PILLBOX: a small, low concrete building that housed guns

RAF: the British air force, known as the Royal Air Force

SIGNAL CORPS: members of the army responsible for communications

SPITFIRE: fighter plane used by British and American air forces

TROOPS: a military group

WIRELESS: British name for radio

Further Reading

BOOKS

Adams, Simon. *DK Eyewitness: World War II*. New York: DK Children, 2014.

Deary, Terry, and Mike Phillips. *Horrible Histories: Blitz*. London: Scholastic, 2009.

Deary, Terry, and Martin Brown. *Horrible Histories: Woeful Second World War*. London: Scholastic, 2011.

Graham, Ian, and David Salariya. *You Wouldn't Want to Be a World War II Pilot*. New York: Franklin Watts, 2009.

Malam, John, and David Salariya. *You Wouldn't Want to Be a Secret Agent During World War II*. New York: Franklin Watts, 2010.

Thompson, Ben. *Guts & Glory: World War II.* New York: Little, Brown Books for Young Readers, 2017.

WEBSITES

history.com/topics/world-war-ii

historyonthenet.com/world-war-two-the-blitz

natgeokids.com/uk/discover/history/general-history /world-war-two

MOVIE

Walt Disney's *Valiant* (2005). (This animated movie tells the story of a group of war pigeons during World War II.)

Katrina Charman

lives in a small village in the middle of Southeast England with her husband and three daughters. Katrina has wanted to be a children's writer ever since she was eleven, when her school teacher set her class the task of writing an epilogue to Roald Dahl's *Matilda*. Her teacher thought her writing was good enough to send to Roald Dahl himself. Sadly, she never got a reply, but the experience ignited her love of reading and writing. She invites you to visit her at katrinacharman.com.

EM*BARK* ON INCREDIBLE HISTORICAL ADVENTURES

WITH

SURVIVAL TAILS!